THE LAST HOMESTEAD

Further Adventures of Denny Caraway, Alaskan Homesteader

Warren Troy

Since
1978

PO Box 221974 Anchorage, Alaska 99522-1974
books@publicationconsultants.com—www.publicationconsultants.com

ISBN 978-1-59433-366-8
eBook ISBN 978-1-59433-364-4
Library of Congress Catalog Card Number: 2013931661

Manufactured in the United States of America.

Chapter One

Denny Caraway was relieved when his gloved hand grasped the wooden latch to the door of his cabin. It had been a long trudge from where he had taken a full-grown bull moose, carrying a front quarter on his pack frame, the straps digging deeply into his shoulders by the time he reached home.

After walking into his small plywood cabin and removing the burden from his back, Caraway started a fire in his cast iron wood stove. He put a lit match to the kindling he'd stacked in the firebox and was pleased when it took the flame well, making it possible to quickly add larger wood. Within minutes he could feel the warmth emanating from the stove, though it would take a solid hour to heat up the cold cabin to a comfortable temperature.

Looking into the tea kettle on the stove top, Denny saw there was enough water in it to make a cup of something hot to drink, once it melted back down from ice and came to a boil.

The meat he had now brought in was the final load, the fifth such trip since he had shot the moose. He considered how the treks back and forth had seemed a lot longer with each successive one, but necessary, nonetheless, to have a good supply of winter food. He had made three trips the first day, wanting to get the meat home as quickly as possible.

Denny regretted making the kill in a thickly-wooded area. He had trailed the moose through the trees into a small clearing that allowed a good clean shot. Though pleased such a large animal would yield plenty of food, he also realized he would not be able to use the snow machine and sled to haul it home, due to the dense undergrowth.

The kill was over a mile away, and while the amount of soft snow on the ground wasn't enough for snowshoeing, it did make walking a hard task. Following his own footprints had made it somewhat easier, but though he was fit, he was weary by the time he was through.

Denny had been living by Lanyard Creek, a branch of the Salcha River, for over three years. Far from civilization, he embraced a rough life in the Alaska bush as the price he had to pay for the peace and solitude he valued so highly.

He was no stranger to remote living, but his first attempt at such an existence had failed, the close proximity to other homesteaders proving to be his downfall. After moving out to this more isolated country, he succeeded in finding the life he needed—a truly solitary existence.

Such self-imposed exile, away from all the everyday conveniences people take for granted, is only possible for a small number of people who have the mental desire, physical capacity, and the sheer grit to exist in the wilderness. Caraway was such a man, though it had taken time for him to clear the debris of his previous mainstream life enough to fully realize this was what he wanted and that he was capable of handling it.

The cabin was nicely warmed now, and the water in the tea kettle was heated to boiling. Denny put a big pinch of Labrador tea into an old, heavy ceramic mug, poured in some boiling water, and put a saucer over the top to let the natural tea steep.

Denny unstrapped the massive moose quarter from his pack rack, and then cut a slot in the smaller lower end between the massive knee tendon and joint. Running a piece of heavy cord through the slot, he picked up the leg and took it outside to where the other moose meat he had brought back was hanging from a cross pole tied between two trees. Tossing the end of the cord over the pole, he hoisted the quarter well clear of the snow-covered ground, tying the line to one of the supporting trees before going back inside to the welcome heat of the stove.

The weary man was finally able to sit back in his cabin, the hot mug of tea in hand, his pacs off and drying near the woodstove. Denny thought about the second trip he had made back to the downed moose.

When he had gotten within sight of it, he stopped to observe the scene in front of him. Caraway saw the snow had been disturbed in a wide area around what remained of the moose carcass, which was not in its original position. There were large, familiar tracks in the snow. With a well-conditioned reflex, he slipped the old Winchester 30-06 off his shoulder, and stood ready.

A few seconds later there was a crashing in the willows, and with a loud roar a young grizzly bear had come charging out directly at him. Reacting instantly, Denny fired a round into the snow in front of the angry bruin, which had the desired effect of turning it away. It continued running, bawling loudly as it went, until it was out of sight and earshot. Denny didn't stand down until the bear had been gone for several minutes.

Though he was glad it hadn't been an older, more determined bear, it could just as well have done him in, badly mauling or killing him. Luckily, it had chosen to leave the kill behind. The bear hadn't been feeding long, and the meat was still in good condition. In the years he had been living in the bush, eight in all, he'd had his run-ins with bears. It was a fact of life in the Alaska wilderness. This incident had, as with previous confrontations, given him chills and goose bumps once it was over.

Though snow had come early—the beginning of November—Denny wasn't worried about dealing with another Alaskan winter. He had plenty of firewood and now meat. The last time he'd gone to Fairbanks for supplies near the end of the previous winter before spring break-up made travel impossible for weeks, he had stocked up on dry provisions such as flour, coffee, and sugar, as well as perishables that needed replacing more often. But soon, he would have to make a run to replace the goods he had used through the spring, summer, and early fall.

He didn't look forward to the journey. It wasn't because of the long day's ride to the Richardson Highway from his homestead, and another long run up the road to Fairbanks. Denny just didn't like having to leave his isolated paradise to go into any crowded center, even Salcha, which had a population of less than 900 inhabitants. But he had long ago learned that if something had to be done, you didn't hang fire over it, you did what was necessary.

For the time being, Denny dropped the idea of another supply run, which could only be made when the snow layer was deep and firm enough to allow him to pull a freighter sled behind his old snowmobile. Right now, he needed to cook and eat some of the fresh moose meat to replenish what he had lost physically on the trail carrying those heavy loads. He had stashed half the back straps in the cooler box, along with the heart and kidneys.

The stove was now hissing hot. Denny lifted the larger of two cast iron skillets hanging on spikes driven into one of the walls. Placing it on the top of the stove, he took the quart jar of cooking oil rendered down from the fat of the black bear he had shot more than a year ago. Sniffing it, he was happy to find it still smelled sweet. Caraway had come to favor bear oil for cooking and baking over any store-bought oils. It didn't seem to saturate whatever he was cooking, and it adds to the food's flavor.

Pouring some oil into the already-heated skillet, he walked over to the sheet metal box made from an old fuel can that he had set into the floor in one corner, for a cooler. Taking out a kidney, he rinsed it off in clear water, and cut it into thick slices with his hunting knife, laying them in the oil bubbling in the hot skillet. The meat immediately began sizzling. Not having eaten since early morning, the sound and smell of frying meat filled his senses, making his mouth water.

Denny found one sorry-looking little onion left in the sack under the counter. After trimming the bad parts away, he still had enough left to cook with the meat in the skillet. He really liked fried onions, especially with fresh game.

It took only a few minutes for the meal to be ready. Placing the food on a plate, he went over to the counter again, lifted the lid to the Dutch oven, and took out a piece of the fry bread he had made several days earlier. A teaspoon of instant coffee in the old mug, boiling water added, and his dinner was complete.

Eating was not normally a special event for Denny in the urban mainstream life he had lived before coming to Alaska. He rarely cooked then, usually eating at a coffee shop or restaurant, so a meal was just a meal. On his remote homestead, the most basic priorities of life regained their true meaning for him. Besides needing to replenish himself, Denny looked forward to meals usually made of what he himself provided. This was one reason Caraway loved the arrival of spring in his northern home. He knew all the edible plants would be coming up soon, adding much needed greens to his plate. He especially liked fiddleheads, immature ferns picked just after they rose up from the forest floor. Steamed and slathered with butter when he had some, plain when he didn't, they were really delicious. Baby nettles were a real tonic in spring, too. But this simple plateful of game meat, onions, and homemade bread would do just fine for now.

Denny paused with a forkful of meat halfway to his mouth. The shrill call of a solitary wolf had sliced through the stillness outside the cabin. Denny walked to the door and opened it slightly, listening intently. Again the call broke out, this time being joined by another voice, and another. Caraway knew he had to get the meat cut up and into his cache right away, remembering an earlier moose he had left too long on the cross pole. He had come out to find over half the meat gone or torn up by sharp fangs and claws. A bear had come in and wreaked havoc on the hanging flesh. Strangely, Denny hadn't heard a sound, nothing awakening him from sleep. It still puzzled him that he hadn't been aware of what was going on.

He hadn't tracked the animal which had ruined his supply that time, knowing the meat was either ruined or digested already, and the idea of shooting the bear that had done the damage didn't sit well with him, unless it came back. It hadn't returned, but Caraway had learned his lesson, and afterwards had stored meat away quickly where nothing could reach it.

Tired as he was, the homesteader set about the task of bringing the partially frozen meat into the cabin, one large section at a time, cutting it into appropriate pieces, and putting it up in game bags he had sewn from heavy cotton muslin. It took him several hours to get it all done, but the moose was now fully processed and stashed in the high cache behind the cabin.

Standing outside the cabin door, admiring the clear, star-filled night sky, Denny had the sense of accomplishment he'd often felt since becoming a homesteader after he had done something to insure his survival, proving his ability to continue the life he had chosen.

Now, it didn't matter if the wolves he'd heard came in the night; his food was secure. Denny went back inside, threw a big piece of seasoned birch in the wood stove, damped it down, and went to bed. Perhaps he would wake up this time if something was prowling outside.

Morning broke clear and a lot colder than the previous day, though darkness would remain until ten. Denny woke up to a cold cabin. He lay in bed a while, not wanting to leave its welcome warmth. His mind settled on the wolf calls from last night. It motivated him to start his day. Slipping out of bed, he pulled on his ratty old insulated Carhartt bibs, a rough wool shirt, and wooly slippers. The fire in the stove still had some glowing red embers, so all he needed to do was toss several pieces of wood in and leave the door and damper open for the fire to be renewed. He checked the teapot. There was plenty of water in it for coffee.

Waiting for the water to heat would take a while, so after shutting the stove door he slipped into his pacs and beaver skin hat and went outside to answer nature's call and breathe in the fresh pure air of an Alaskan morning.

The sight of several sets of wolf prints brought him out of his morning reverie. They were a couple dozen feet from the cabin, and about the same distance from the empty meat pole.

Then he found markings in the snow suggesting that at least two of the wolves had lain facing the cabin door, if he was interpreting them correctly, as if they were waiting for him to come out. Denny pondered why the wolves would do such a thing, but he had long ago learned not to assume anything in the bush. The unexpected was always possible, the unexplainable always around. The cold was really soaking into him now, so he went back in to warm up and eat breakfast.

Chapter Two

A solid foot of snow fell about a week after Denny had stored his moose meat. Now he could make a run to restock his dwindling supplies. The night after the snow fell, Caraway sat at his little hand-sawed spruce table, making a list of what he needed.

His first homesteading location hadn't made things difficult when it came to resupplying. He had been well within reach of the stores and shops in the town of Hazel, making the trip in a few hours in winter or summer. But now, his home on Lanyard Creek required a much longer ride on his snowmobile to get to the road system, coming out at the little community of Salcha, and then a run up to Fairbanks by pick-up, to get everything he needed.

The homesteader double-checked his list: foodstuffs; clothing to replace worn-out pants, socks, and shirts; some tools; and parts for his chainsaw. As always, the list included some treats: a big bag of the licorice whips he loved, some chocolate chip cookies, peanut butter, and a small bottle of good bourbon for special occasions. He also needed to haul in twenty-five to thirty gallons of gas, and five gallons of kerosene for his lantern.

Denny had originally bought a supposedly heavy-duty plastic freighting sled for hauling, but it had lasted only a winter and a half before breaking up on a rough stretch of trail halfway home, with about 500 pounds of supplies in it. He'd made repeated runs to get all the goods to the cabin, carrying what he could in the snowmobile's rear rack and on the back portion of its seat. It had taken most of the night to get it all in to his homestead. A week later, he rode back out and drove up to Fairbanks to buy a sturdier sled.

Denny had found the hauling sled he needed in an outdoor supply store in Fairbanks. It had a heavy aluminum frame and body, and four skis, the two in front swiveling with the hitch bar for better handling. It had been built for expedition and rescue work, and was a fine rig. He had to pay a steep price for it, but Caraway knew it could easily handle a heavy load, and would last as long as he did. It was worth the trip to find such a great piece of equipment.

Now, he was prepared for another run up to Fairbanks. The skidoo was all fueled up and ready to go. The sled held his emergency pack, snowshoes, and six empty five-gallon plastic gasoline containers.

The weather was clear and crisp, almost fifteen degrees below zero. Denny had experienced much colder weather, so this was no deterrent. The temperature had made the snow perfect for riding. Denny hated to run over wet, clingy snow, especially with a loaded sled, which could bog down easily and be a rough go to get unstuck.

His Skidoo came to life with two pulls on the starter cord. He marveled that the twenty-year-old machine still ran so well, even in sub-zero weather, and he dreaded the time when it would ultimately wear out. If he could, he'd try to find the same kind of machine to replace it when necessary.

Denny always got what he called "trail jitters," a mixture of excitement and nervousness, just before every ride. He never knew what lay waiting for him amongst the hills and valleys and in the forest. Still, he was always glad to start his journey and experience the adventure of the trail.

Dressed for the trail, the 30-06 slung on his shoulder, Denny mounted the snowmobile. He pressed down on the thumb throttle and the machine jumped forward as if it too was looking forward to the run. If all went well, by late afternoon Caraway would reach his destination.

Chapter Three

Charlie Brady owned and operated the North Star Cafe, in the town of Salcha on Richardson Highway. He had been an Alaska State Trooper for twenty years, the last thirteen as a wildlife officer, before retiring in this area of Alaska where he had always been assigned.

Brady had come up from Montana to work for the troopers, with a powerful curiosity about Alaska. Now, twenty years later, his interest had not diminished, and he still enjoyed traveling in the areas he used to patrol when investigating illegal hunting cases and other bad behavior in the deep bush country. Charlie still loved to make snowmobile runs on the area's established trails and other stretches not so well known to outsiders, and he hunted for caribou and moose when he could get away from the cafe.

Right now, he was hoping somebody would come in for a cup of coffee just to break the monotony. He knew from the get-go the cafe would not be a big money-making proposition, and held none of the exciting times his trooper duties provided. But he had a comfortable cabin behind the place, and everything was paid for, so he was well set-up. Besides, he wouldn't be happy living elsewhere.

Looking out through the small front door window, he saw the red in the outdoor thermometer well down in the bottom of the tube which held it captive. It looked to be about twenty below zero. Cold, but he had seen the temperatures in this country down past fifty-five below a time or two.

Before he turned away from the window, he saw someone pull up on an old Skidoo snowmobile, with a big metal sled trailing behind. He could see a set of long, old-fashioned wood and sinew snowshoes sticking up from within the sled's bed. The man had on a beaver skin trapper hat, rabbit fur mitts, a heavy pullover parka, and a pair of fancy-looking expedition boots. Snow goggles hung around his neck.

Charlie knew him, and went over to the counter to pour the soon-to-be requested cup of coffee. He tapped a dash of cinnamon into it, knowing the man would want it that way, and waited.

A minute later, the door opened and the traveler slipped in, quickly pulling the door shut behind him. He had a heavy beard and mustache, most of which, along with his eyebrows, were covered with hoarfrost from the cold trail. From out of this icy, furry countenance pierced a pair of pale blue eyes some people found a little unnerving in their unwavering directness. In truth, the man's way of looking at things seemed a little too intense for most, but Charlie knew Denny Caraway lived in the bush, and his life, though surely having some light moments, was mostly serious business, so being focused and very observant was a matter of survival.

"Hello, Caraway," Charlie greeted the woodsman.

"Hello yourself, Officer Brady," responded the wild-looking guy.

On the surface, there seemed little friendship between the two, judging from their scant words, but it was a matter of mutual respect for one another that kept their conversation brief. The two men each had an innate understanding of the other's experiences and knowledge of the bush, so few words were needed.

Brady knew Caraway to be a conscientious woodsman and subsistence hunter, living on a secluded homestead by a remote creek. Brady had paid him several visits over the years Caraway had been living there. For his part, Caraway knew Brady to be a fair but no-nonsense wildlife officer, an honest, straightforward man who knew the country well and had been dedicated to his work. They had taken part in several search and rescue missions together out in Denny's home territory. The first time, when Brady came to ask his help, Caraway gave it without question or pay.

One of the few times Brady saw Caraway smile was right after Charlie had retired and opened the North Star. Denny had come by in his big dual-wheeled truck and, with a serious expression, asked Charlie if the Department was going to be happy, knowing he was moonlighting. Brady was just going to tell him he was retired, when he saw a twinkle in Denny's eyes and the slightest twitch of his lip, which was Caraway's normal version of a smile. Denny was already a regular at the cafe, at least as regular as a remote home-steader can be, living way the heck and gone off the road system.

Charlie reached under the counter and gave Caraway a dry, clean cloth towel. The big oil-burning heat stove was doing its job, quickly thawing Caraway's arctic face and boots, leaving a good-sized puddle on the floor around his feet. After Denny wiped the dampness off his face, he cleaned up the water on the floor, handing Charlie back the now dingy towel, with a nod.

When a pair of road travelers came in, Denny left Charlie to his business. Before seating himself at a table, he picked up the Anchorage newspaper from the counter to see what foolishness was going on in the larger world. Scanning through the day-old rag, he saw a small article on the death of a well-known shop owner in Hazel, Alaska. He became seriously interested in the story when he saw it was Ed Gundross, the man who had helped and befriended Denny when he first began homesteading up past the head of Long Bay, outside Hazel. The story might not have been written up in the Anchorage paper, except Ed had been on a search and rescue mission looking for the missing son of a successful Anchorage businessman, when he'd had an accident on his snow machine, rolled down a slope, and crashed into a tree. The heavy machine had come down on top of him, killing Ed instantly.

Ed had sold Denny his first chainsaws and a hand-held wood-milling tool to be mounted on one of them to make dimensional lumber for building his cabin, and sundry items needed for living out in the bush. Ed had even guided Denny out to the land he intended to homestead. Caraway had been green as grass, a cheechako, when he first started out. Ed had taken him under his experienced wing and they became good friends. But now, living up Lanyard Creek as he was, Denny was out of touch with people for long periods of time, though he sent Ed a Christmas card every year with a little note about what he had been up to. A card this year would apparently not be necessary. Denny wasn't religious by nature, but he took a moment to bow his head and say a little prayer for Ed.

With the two customers sitting contentedly over mugs of hot coffee, Charlie noticed Denny with his head bowed and he went over to Caraway's table, waited for him to finish, then asked if he was okay. Denny told Charlie about Ed's passing and their friendship.

Charlie said, "Are you going to his memorial? Would you be able to get there in time?"

"I think I'd better, Charlie," Denny told him. "It wouldn't sit right with me if I didn't. I haven't been down there in, well, since I came up here to homestead three years ago. Yeah, I have to do it. My supplies can wait a few days."

Instead of ordering some food, Denny put his parka on, nodded to Charlie, and headed out the door. He stood outside for a moment letting his mind clear before putting his hat and gloves on, starting up the Skidoo, and riding down the side of the road. He was going about a mile south of the cafe to a small mobile home he had been given when he purchased the ten acres of wilderness land he lived on from George Levine. It was his base of operations during the times he came out from the homestead, and Denny kept his truck there. A neighbor whose home was just north of where the trailer was located kept an eye on the trailer for Denny and started up the truck every two weeks while Caraway was in the bush.

Denny had bought the truck when he was leaving his first homestead. Leaving was the last thing he had wanted to do. He had spent years building his cabin, and establishing himself. In that first remote location, he had become the man he needed to be to survive even farther from civilization, deeper in the bush. He had come to realize his first homesteading experience was training to be a committed homesteader, without the nearby lifelines of town and other people the first location had provided him.

Until he had made that first attempt, he didn't know he would be able to exist and thrive in such wild, isolated country. But homesteading had completely replaced his earlier mainstream life, which had ultimately proven to be totally unsatisfying for him. Denny had found life in the woods fulfilling, and it enabled him to discover his true character.

Several homesteaders living near him had ruined things when they began developing the forest right next to Denny's land, which would destroy his hard won sanctuary. The situation had driven him to a more isolated piece of land, which had turned out to be the proper place for him. He hoped nothing would change, and was prepared to do whatever was necessary to keep this homestead, and the life he had built. This time there would be no giving up his home, not for any reason.

The truck started right up when Caraway turned the key to warm the engine. He went into the trailer to gather a few pieces of "civilized" clothing from the bedroom closet. Briefly looking at his face in the bathroom mirror, he noticed how overgrown his beard and hair were, shrugged, turned off the light, and went into the little living room. Reaching under the couch cushion, he pulled out a short-barreled .38 caliber revolver and put it in his parka's side pocket. Taking his .44 magnum revolver from its holster, Denny wiped it down with a paper towel and put it where the .38 had been. He hung the big pistol's holster and belt in the broom closet. Setting the heater to low, and turning off the living room light, he stepped out and locked the door.

The pickup was ready to roll, the heater filling the cab with welcome warmth. Denny got into the truck, pulled his parka off and put the little revolver in the glove box. He didn't feel comfortable without a firearm within easy reach, a direct effect of wilderness living. He'd had to draw his .44 several times in touchy situations with bears in the eight years he'd homesteaded, but had never needed to shoot it except to scare the problem away. But, all would be lost if he needed it and the pistol wasn't there. Carrying the .38 on the road and in town was for the same reason, to be prepared if a need for defending his life arose.

The big pickup truck Denny was driving down to Hazel was a practical piece of equipment, pure and simple. Unlike many who owned such a vehicle merely for what it symbolized, Caraway had made good use of its hauling capabilities, such as bringing the big freighter sled home and carrying large amounts of supplies and fuel. It had served him well. He had thought of putting a camper on the back, but realized he had more use for the open bed, although in winter it held a large mass of snow to be shoveled out after a good fall. The neighbor, Elliot, who watched the trailer, shoveled the bed out regularly in winter, or asked his grandson Drew to do it.

As was usually the case, being on the open road allowed Denny's mind to run free. Though he paid attention to his driving, Caraway didn't have to focus his mind on the numerous, potentially dangerous situations traveling in the bush held in store.

Denny hit the brakes, the stable truck sliding only slightly on the icy road surface. A big cow moose had decided to make its way across the highway at the precise moment Denny came driving by. Caraway had spotted the animal instantly, though someone with less experience might not have seen it coming out of the trees as quickly as he had. For a full minute after the moose had disappeared into the trees on the opposite side of the road Denny waited, in case it had a calf or two following behind. Moose in general don't understand the danger vehicles running down a road at high speed holds for them, and young moose are even less aware.

Continuing on his way, Denny felt some deep hunger pangs. He hadn't eaten at the North Star Cafe as he had planned, the news about his friend Ed putting him off his feed. Pulling into a small clearing by the roadside, he reached behind the seat and pulled up a bag he had made from last year's moose's hide. It had a shoulder strap and a flap over the top of the bag, a big button he had carved from a piece of caribou antler holding it closed. Opening it, he took out a piece of folded up cotton cloth holding some jerky he had made. He also took out another piece of cloth containing the fry bread he always enjoyed.

Denny had been given the recipe by an Athabascan Indian fellow he had met while caribou hunting in an area southwest of his homestead. The man had ridden up on a big new snowmobile towing a sled loaded with several field-dressed caribou. Denny welcomed him and offered a cup of coffee, a tradition in Alaska when someone came to visit, no matter where you happened to be.

The man had shared some meat sandwiches he had with him made of a rich-tasting, chewy flatbread. Denny asked him about it and the Indian had told him it was fry bread, a real staple where he came from. He told Denny how to make it, a simple recipe, but, he told him if he didn't put a good pinch of salt in it and cook it in a cast iron skillet, it wouldn't taste right. Denny never forgot the advice. He thought the bear oil he used for cooking made it even tastier. Fry bread had become a staple in his diet too.

Chapter Four

It took a long day to get to Hazel, and even though it wasn't full winter yet, December just coming in, daylight was in short supply already, and he arrived well after dark. He went right over to the old Hazel Shores motel, a funky little place dating back to the 1960s, run by an older woman named Ruthie Bennett, who could have passed for the sister of Denny's old friend, Hazel O'Mara, who had passed away years before.

Hazel had been one of the first permanent white inhabitants in the area of South Central Alaska that eventually became the little hamlet of Hazel, named after her. Her husband Benny was the other. Benny had died in the 1970s, when a gruesome car accident put him over the bluff above the inlet adjacent to Hazel. He had crashed far below, upon the rocky shore. After his death, Hazel had stayed in the little town with her daughter Gwen, running a great little cafe.

Denny had really liked Hazel, coming to appreciate her personality and way of dealing with life. He'd had a brief intimate relationship with her daughter Gwen which had ended when Hazel died, because Gwen needed to make big adjustments after her passing. She and Caraway had grown close, but neither of them had wanted a full commitment at the time. They'd enjoyed one another's company, but it had gone no farther. For his part, living on his homestead was Caraway's main priority. When it was clear she needed to move on in a direction that wouldn't include him, Denny had accepted the change and continued his solitary life.

Ruthie was glad to see Denny after his three-year absence from the area. She dragged him by one arm into her cozy kitchen in the back of the motel office, poured him a cup of coffee, and insisted he tell her what he had been up to. While Denny wasn't big on conversation, he was glad to see Ruthie again, and willing to tell her about his new homestead and what life was like there.

In turn, Ruthie told him all the gossip about Hazel since he'd been gone. He found most of what Ruthie told him mildly interesting until she told him Gwen O'Mara was back in Hazel. She had married an old high school flame just before Denny had left, but the flame had apparently died quickly when the husband found out Gwen was not a woman one could expect to be obedient to a husband's every whim, which is what he demanded. Gwen was her mother's child, strong and independent. She finally dumped him and was living back in her mother's old cabin. Gwen was managing the Log Cabin Cafe again, for the current owners.

The news about Gwen sparked some interest on Denny's part, and he planned to visit her and say hello, but he knew it probably wouldn't be the same between them. Time, distance, and life had surely done their part to change things.

Ruthie talked to Denny about Ed Gundross' memorial, the when and where. She saddened visibly when she discussed it with him, as she had known Ed for many years and was a good friend.

Denny got the key to a room from Ruthie and settled in. He ordered a small pizza to be delivered from the local pizzeria, and lay back on the bed letting the day wind down. When the pizza arrived, he was surprised at how much he enjoyed it. He hadn't tasted one in years. Then he took a long shower, letting the hot water soak into his bones. The chlorinated smell was unpleasant, but well worth putting up with for the shower's soothing qualities. There was a TV in the room, but Caraway didn't even consider turning it on.

Denny missed his homestead routines already — starting and keeping the wood stove going, getting fresh sweet water from Lanyard Creek, and cooking his own food. He mused over the way his priorities had changed and simplified. He was totally content with a homesteading life despite the hardships and inconveniences. Even a small pizza was an uncommon and unnecessary thing.

Denny looked at himself in the mirror on the motel room wall. He was leaner and tougher than he had ever been, in really good shape for a man going on fifty. He wasn't impressed with himself, but was glad to observe that, barring any major accidents, he would probably be able to continue home-steading for a good long time.

The pizza was starting to make trouble with his innards, the cheese, tomato sauce, and the plain white dough not common fare for him. He hoped things wouldn't get messy. Fortunately, he slept through the night with no major digestive disturbances. Caraway was hungry when he woke up and craving a cup of coffee or two. Dressing in the one clean change of clothes he had with him, he drove right over to the Log Cabin Cafe.

When he walked in, there were several of the same customers who had always frequented the place at breakfast time when he was still living in the area. He nodded to them as he had done many times in the past and they nodded back, as though nothing had changed or was out of place. When he looked around, there was Gwen holding a coffee pot, looking at him with a stunned expression. After a moment she said, "Take a seat anywhere, I'll be right with you."

Denny sat at the window table he had always favored. Looking at the menu, he saw it hadn't changed much either, except for the prices. He would order what he usually did. Gwen came up and poured him a cup. He could smell the slight scent of cinnamon in the coffee. Taking a sniff, he smiled and said to her, "I'm glad to see some things are still the same."

"Some things, Mr. Caraway, but not everything. Life has a way of doing that to us."

"Without a doubt, Gwen, but you look well."

Gwen's eyes flickered for a moment, some fleeting emotion passing through them. It wasn't lost on Denny, though he chose not to play on it.

"I came down for Ed's memorial service. Are you going?"

"That's a foolish question, Denny Caraway. You know I knew him my whole life."

A few customers glanced up at Gwen's sharp response, then quickly looked back at their plates.

There was an irritated note in Gwen's voice Caraway couldn't miss. So, he decided to end the conversation and just order his breakfast. Gwen slipped her order book into her apron pocket, and went behind the counter to cook.

For the rest of the time, Denny and Gwen didn't speak at all. It felt awkward, so Denny wolfed down his food, didn't ask for a second cup of java, left money on the table, and walked out. As he was getting into his truck, Gwen came out and walked over to him.

"I'm sorry Denny, it was a surprise to see you out of the blue after all this time. It caught me off guard. I wonder if you'd like to have dinner with me after the service this afternoon and catch up?"

Denny chose his words carefully. "I'm sorry I didn't let you know I was coming. It was a quick decision, when I read about Ed, instead of going up to Fairbanks for supplies as I had planned. Besides, I didn't even know you were back in Hazel until Ruthie told me."

Gwen smiled and said, "Leave it to Ruthie to broadcast the world's news at the drop of a hat."

"Tell you what, Gwen, how about if I come by the cafe for lunch tomorrow to visit, before I head north again."

"No, that's okay, Denny, maybe we just better leave it alone."

"Okay, Gwen, you take care of yourself. If I get down this way again, I'll let you know ahead of time."

"Sure Denny, you take it easy."

Gwen O'Mara turned and walked away, back into the warmth of the cafe. Denny started up the truck and headed to the motel. He made himself accept how things were, though just then, he felt as if he was in a country western song. Even though they'd see each other at the service and reception, he knew they'd keep some distance, which was probably for the best.

Denny hung around the motel until it was time to go to Ed's service at the little church east of town, the one Gundross had attended all his years in Hazel. The minister there kept his words brief, letting Ed's friends speak for him.

Denny recognized nearly everyone who spoke, and a lot of the people in the pews. Glancing around, he saw one face he had no desire to see. Bucky Waters was sitting in a far back corner. Denny faced forward again, an old familiar heat starting to build in his neck. He forced himself to calm down and listen to the testimonials. When the service was over, he stood and turned to leave, and saw Waters was already gone, which was fine with him. Seeing his old homesteading neighbor and nemesis was unexpected, and all the bad feelings between them had come to the surface again. He had hoped he'd never see him again. After all, it was Waters who had caused him to leave his first homestead by developing the land right across the tundra from him, which would ruin Caraway's wilderness sanctuary. Another neighbor, Monty Leer, had also been involved, but because Leer was a decent man, Denny harbored no grudge against him.

Gwen was at the service too, of course, and as Denny had figured, they simply cast each other a quick glance and nothing more passed between them.

Caraway drove over to where the reception was being held, at Ed's old house, which had been a homestead until the town had grown up around it. Ed had added on to the one-room structure, until it had become a five-room home with indoor plumbing. You could see where it had grown out of the old cabin, which was still visible at one end of the building. He and his wife, who had passed away before Denny had met Ed, had lived there for many years, raising their son Jeff.

There were at least fifty people there, including Ed's son, who had flown up from Seattle to take care of the arrangements and Ed's estate. Denny introduced himself after his old friend Walt, who had bought Denny's first homestead, pointed Ed's son out to him. Jeff Gundross smiled and said his father had spoken about him a number of times.

"He told me, Mr. Caraway, you reminded him of the old-time homesteaders he had met, if you don't mind me saying so. Dad said you were a decent man of many parts, as he put it, and he told me he missed your company a great deal after you had moved away."

Denny thanked the personable young man for telling him, and they shook hands.

Denny sat down on the couch in the living room, a cup of hot coffee in his hand. Through the screen of people in front of him, he noticed Bucky Waters standing by a table covered with dishes and bowls of home-made food people had brought. Waters wasn't aware of him.

Caraway became disgusted watching him. Waters had a plate piled high and a mouthful of something he was chewing on. Denny knew Bucky and Ed hadn't gotten on well. And yet Gundross, being the kind of man he was, let Bucky come in and buy what he needed for his homestead needs, as long as Waters had cash to pay for the supplies. Bucky had a chip on his shoulder over that demand, even though he'd previously given Ed one bad check and had taken too long to pay off the tab Gundross had graciously allowed him. So, Waters being there stuffing his face, was really a cheap shot. The final straw for Denny was when he saw Waters stuffing a couple of small rolls in his pocket.

Rising from the couch, he walked over to Bucky, pulled the plate out of his hand and, setting it on the table, told him quietly and firmly, "I think you're through here, Waters."

Waters almost lost the food in his mouth when Denny made his presence known. A slight shudder ran through him a moment after he saw Denny. Through his half-eaten food, he managed to say, "You miserable bastard," before turning and walking out the front door.

Denny was so angry, he had to go outside for a while to cool off. He went out the back door, not wanting to have another confrontation with Waters, knowing he had little control of himself at that moment.

Five minutes later, a calmer Caraway came back into the house, said his farewells to a number of people he knew, and headed out to his pickup. He started the truck to warm it up and sat listening to some music on the radio, lost in thought and memories.

Suddenly the driver's side door was yanked open and Bucky Waters lashed out at him. The punch caught Denny off guard, landing square on the side of his jaw. Dazed, Denny swiveled around in his seat and shoved Bucky away with his feet, giving himself time to step out of the truck. Bucky seemed a little surprised, expecting his sucker punch to put Denny out, standing there, not knowing what to do next.

Shaking his head to clear it, Caraway looked straight into Bucky's eyes. Bucky slumped visibly when Denny lined up on him. Taking two steps forward, Denny faked a punch to Bucky's head, causing him to throw his arms up to protect himself, and Denny gave him a hard shot to the gut. When Bucky dropped his hands to cover his stomach, Denny gave him a hard right hand to the jaw. The punch put him down, but Denny lifted him up again and gave him another good one to the nose. He wanted to make sure Bucky didn't forget his error in judgment.

Standing there, feeling strangely calm, Denny said, "Now we're done." Bucky just grunted and lay still on the ground.

Looking to his left, Denny saw a dozen people, including Gwen, standing outside Ed's front door. He noticed most of them were smiling. Bucky Waters was no stranger to any of them. They knew all about the bad deeds he had done over the years, and were not sorry to see him get some pay back.

Gwen walked up to Caraway, the smile off her face. She stood a foot away from Bucky, totally ignoring him. Looking into Denny's eyes, she said, "Feel better now?"

"More than you know, Gwen."

"Don't be so sure of that, Mr. Caraway. You forget, I've known him longer than you and I'm not sorry to see him get taken down. I know my mom would be proud of you. The least I can do is offer you some dinner, if you're interested."

"That sounds good to me. Meet you at the cafe?"

"What, did you forget the way to my cabin?"

"'Course not. I'll see you around seven."

"Fine, and bring a bottle of red wine."

When Denny woke up, it was already light. He was surprised to have slept so late, usually getting up before the sun. Gwen was gone, and a little note on her kitchen table told him she was glad to have spent time with him, but had to open the cafe. "Come in for breakfast, unless you sleep till noon, in which case it'll be for lunch."

Denny smiled. It had been an unexpected and very satisfying evening. Though the isolated life up north was fine for him, being with Gwen had certainly been special, a pleasant departure from his normally serious life. Combined with finally having definite closure with Bucky Waters, it had taken some of the sadness away from giving Ed his send-off, and Caraway was sure, wherever Ed was, he had no objections.

Having another meal at the Log Cabin Cafe brought back some of the good feelings he'd had in Hazel while building his original homestead. A trip to town for whatever reason always included meals at the cafe. Even before his relationship with Gwen O'Mara had become intimate, he always looked forward to time spent there. He'd never had any real traditions in his earlier life, living in Reno, but coming to Alaska and homesteading had awakened the desire to do so. Being a regular at the cafe seemed fitting.

Denny had ordered his usual breakfast. He found the flavor and quality of the food was still the same as when Gwen's mom still ran the place.

He didn't have much conversation with Gwen this time. They were content to just hang around each other, Caraway enjoying his meal and her company as he used to, watching her take care of the customers. Knowing Denny was there made her normal routine more enjoyable.

She did ask him about his solitary life, and he told her how it was for him, living so far out and away, and how it differed from his first bush home.

Time came for him to leave. He walked up to the counter to pay his bill, but Gwen refused the money. Denny gave her a long look, a momentary little smile playing across his weathered face. He touched her cheek, then left the cafe. He wasn't aware of the little thrill that ran through her after the slight contact. Cranking up his truck, he left Hazel once again.

Chapter Five

Denny still loved the drive north from Hazel. Fact was, he never tired of traveling anywhere in Alaska, be it by truck, snow machine, or by shank's mare. He was always ready to explore new places. Maybe that was why he often broke new trails when he already had one cut to get to the same place, to have a different route to travel along. When he wasn't busy with all the chores necessary to survive out on the land, he explored the area around his homestead, often staying out overnight, loving the stillness of the forest, listening for the occasional sound of some animal passing by. Though he'd had unexpected non-human visitors to his camps, he'd always known how to handle the situations. Sleeping out under the trees, he'd wake up numerous times to look around, listen and even sniff the air. Denny was truly a forest dweller, like any other denizen of the woods.

He arrived in Anchorage about five hours later, having driven a little faster than he usually did, in spite of the slick road surface. Denny wanted to gather his needed supplies as quickly as possible and head back to his 'stead. Despite the events of the past several days, he missed his little plywood cabin. Coming up from the south, he could shop in Anchorage, then head straight back to Salcha.

Denny filled all the plastic gas cans and his truck's tanks prior to leaving Anchorage. He'd already loaded the bed of his truck with bags and packages of foodstuffs not readily available outside city limits. It was all pretty common fare — beans, coffee, flour, sugar, and such. Of course, he included some treats, several packages of Oreos and a bag of his favorite sweet, licorice whips.

One thing he added was a hand grain grinder, bought at a health food store in lower Anchorage, and two five-gallon buckets full of whole wheat grain.

He intended to grind his own flour to make fry bread, and was going to try making real loaves of bread, too.

On the way out, almost by reflex, Denny pulled off to check out an outdoor supply store. He didn't really need anything, but wanted to see what they had. It turned out they had several things he could use.

Denny found a pair of what were called Arctic Expedition gloves. They were well made, tough and water proof, and had special insulation that was thin, yet warm. Denny told the salesman he preferred mitts over gloves for use in extremely cold weather. The guy assured him the gloves would keep his hands warm in any weather Alaska presented, and Denny took him at his word.

The other piece of equipment that interested him was a sleeping bag. Though he had a good down mummy bag, he never liked the style, preferring more room to move around, for comfort and in case he needed to get out of it quickly.

This bag looked really good, and had a little insulated cover for his head. It was extremely light and very expensive. Denny considered whether or not to spend that much money, until he recalled what Ed Gundross had told him — buy the best gear possible, because it just might save his life sometime. He bought the bag, and the gloves.

Glad to get out of the city, Denny continued north on the Glenn Highway, the need to get home urging him on. A few times along the way, he thought about the events of the previous several days. He'd had a much better time than he'd anticipated, and was feeling good about life in general. He'd expected a long drive, and not much more.

As always, when he had to be away Caraway had mental images of his little homestead waiting for him to come back. Running up the Glenn and then onto the Richardson Highway heading towards Salcha, he drew designs in his mind for the garden he planned on starting in spring for growing basic vegetables — potatoes, carrots, onions, turnips, and perhaps some cabbage and lettuce too. He'd bought seed in Anchorage. It would certainly enhance his diet to have some produce to last into the winter months.

He also put his thoughts towards building the log cabin he had been considering for a while. Though the plywood cabin he had now was serving him well enough, it had some shortcomings. Denny craved the look and feel of a snug log home. He had loved living in the one he had bought from George Whiting where he began his homesteading life. Though it had needed lots of work, the small log structure had been perfect for him. He had come to realize the new frame cabin he'd built while living in the bush outside Hazel had really been more than he needed. Perhaps his mind, at the time, was still oriented to the mainstream life he had been living before coming to Alaska, when he believed in the theory of bigger is better. He now knew what was really necessary to exist in wild country. A smaller cabin was easier to keep warm, requiring less wood and therefore less rigorous labor. He'd learned there was much he just plain didn't need to still be well supplied and happy.

Seeing the road sign announcing Salcha, Denny actually got a little bubble of excitement as the old mobile home came into view, a thin covering of snow crowning its roof. Being in Salcha meant he was back in his own territory. Though he spent little time in it, the trailer was invaluable for keeping some of his goods safe and sound.

He saw his neighbor Elliot had plowed the driveway and side yard, as he always did in winter, despite being in his late seventies. He was a decent man, and a long time Alaskan. Living in a small rural community, Elliot knew the value of good neighbors.

Denny brought him some fresh meat whenever he came out from the homestead, and an occasional six pack of beer from the Salcha grocery store. Elliot wasn't much of a drinker, but he enjoyed a brew from time to time. The old fellow had refused any money for his help, and Denny was grateful for all he did.

Caraway went into the trailer and found it to be above freezing. He had started up the propane heater and set it on low before leaving, planning on staying there when he got back from Hazel. He wanted to head out for the 'stead in the morning before first light, to make use of what light there was at this late time of year.

Denny took a plastic container of frozen moose stew from the refrigerator's little freezer and set it out to thaw, putting it on a little box right in front of the heater outlet. He went back outside after putting on his parka and new gloves to start loading up the big sled with what could remain outside without freezing. He put the full fuel cans up front, then loaded the bags and packages of dry goods in next. There was enough to make a full layer in the sled, which would keep things from sliding around while on the trail. He pulled a heavy canvas tarp over the top in case of snow, and took the perishable things inside to keep in the fridge until morning. The new gloves had kept his hands warm indeed.

The rest of the evening went peacefully. Denny ate the moose stew, played some quiet music and sat back on the couch to relax a while before hitting the sack.

The man never liked leaving his homestead, knowing the longer he was away, the greater the chance something could happen to the place. Well, tomorrow would come soon enough and by late afternoon he'd be home and everything would be fine.

Chapter Six

It was still pitch black when Denny went outside the next morning, a big bowl of oatmeal and several cups of instant coffee in his belly. He slipped the powerful headlamp over his hat and switched the beam on. His breath was coming out as white clouds in the bitter cold air.

It took a little while to load the rest of the goods into the sled, and he went inside to shut down the trailer down.

He had slipped the little .38 revolver back under the couch cushion and retrieved his trusty old .44. Caraway was used to the weight of the big pistol. It had become a natural thing for him to have it hanging on his hip.

He made sure the truck was locked up, then turned his attention to the snow machine parked under the carport. Pulling the tarp off, he primed the carburetor and gave two good pulls on the starter rope. It didn't start right up as it usually did. Several more pulls and the engine came to life, though reluctantly. A seed of doubt sprouted in Denny's mind.

On the way out from the cabin it had started up all right and ran well until about half way down the trail to Salcha. It was then the machine had slowed down, feeling tight, so Denny had stopped and shut it off. He lifted the hood to check things out visually, and saw nothing unusual or out of place. After starting it again and riding for a while it seemed okay, but he paid close attention to the sound and feel of the engine as he continued on.

Mounting the Skidoo, he gave it some throttle to run it over to the sled and hitch it up. Denny rode it only a few yards when the engine made several loud clunking noises and stopped.

Fully concerned now, he pulled on the starter cord several times. Instead of coming to life, the engine simply went clank, clank, clank! Denny knew some major metal part had given it up. It was obvious to him that an engine rebuild on a machine this old wasn't the way to go. The time he dreaded had arrived: a new snowmobile was necessary.

After staring at the Skidoo for a long minute, feeling as if he had lost another friend, Denny got the tarp and gently laid it over the now defunct snowmobile.

After bringing the perishables back into the trailer, the frustrated homesteader cranked up the heater again and sat dejectedly on the couch, knowing he'd be making the drive to Fairbanks after all, instead of heading home.

Denny was not a man who liked being forced into situations where he had no real choice in the matter, but he knew he had to do what needed doing, so Fairbanks in the morning it would be. Throwing a blanket over himself, he drifted off to sleep on the couch.

The drive north was uneventful and boring. The first shop he stopped at in Fairbanks didn't have the type of snowmobile he needed, and he didn't like the people at the second one. He had only one more choice in dealerships, and he went there hoping to find what he needed.

When he went in, a young guy wearing a racing jersey came up to him and said, "Man, did you come at a good time if you want a hot mountain sled!"

Caraway raised his hand, palm towards the young hot shot, which silenced him immediately. Denny saw an older guy at a desk in a corner, calmly sipping on a cup of what was presumably coffee and reading a newspaper. Walking over to the desk and waiting for him to look up, Denny told the man he needed a reliable snowmobile to get out to his homestead pulling a heavy load, saying, "I don't need anything fancy with a thousand horsepower."

"Well," the man replied, setting his cup down, "I really don't do much selling."

Glancing at the kid who was still giving him a questioning look, Denny told the fellow at the desk, "I need someone who understands what I really need, and you look like him."

Sizing Denny up, noting his seasoned parka and boots, the heavy beard, and the unblinking direct gaze, he said, "Come out back with me. I think I have just what you need."

Putting on a heavy coat and hat, he walked Denny out through the service area door with "Employees Only" painted on it, through the shop and out to the back lot. There were at least thirty different machines of all styles there. The man walked right up to a particular rig, and pulled off the cover.

Denny was keen to see that it appeared to be a newer version of his old one, but it had a wider stance between the skis, a longer track, and a taller, wider windshield, which would make trail riding in cold weather more bearable. It didn't seem as fancy and radical as most of the newer machines. It looked just right.

The salesman primed the carburetor with three pushes of the primer rod, and pulled the starter cord twice. The engine came right to life and after warming up a bit, sounded as if all it wanted to do was run, like a good sled dog. The man told Denny to take it for a spin, pointing out a nice area behind the shop to try it out. It took Denny only a few minutes to know this was exactly what he wanted. It was very stable and pulled stronger than he had expected.

Coming back in, Denny said it ran fine, and asked what the new machine cost.

"Oh, this isn't new; it's about three years old and has a little less than four hundred miles on it. It's my own Tundra II. I have two other machines I use a whole lot more than this one, and I think this is just what you need, so I'm willing to sell it to you for a fair price. I'll throw in some engine oil, a spare belt, and a headlamp bulb. The cover comes with it too."

Caraway was amazed that the immaculate snowmobile wasn't new, and without hesitation stuck out his hand and they shook on the deal. When the man told him the machine had reverse, it was frosting on the cake. He thought back to the number of times he'd had to get unstuck by clearing snow and yanking his old machine around by hand, and was pleased.

The money and paperwork all settled, and the machine slid into the bed of his truck, Denny shook hands once again with the decent fellow he had been dealing with, and asked him how long he had worked there.

"I opened the shop about twelve years ago, and it's been a good business ever since."

Acknowledging the owner's statement, Denny nodded, thanked him again, and headed south to Salcha, looking forward to his first ride on the new snowmobile.

Denny drove back to his trailer, unloaded the machine, checked and found the gas tank and oil reservoir were full, and went into the trailer to spend the night.

Early the next morning, he hitched his new snow machine up to the heavily-loaded sled. Besides the supplies he had bought, all his necessary trail gear was stashed in the sled and in the large rear cargo rack on the Tundra. It made up quite a load. Thinking, "Let's see how it goes," Denny pressed down on the thumb throttle and the bright yellow machine pulled forward with ease. Denny was finally on his way home.

Chapter Seven

Denny was happy with his new ride. It seemed to be able to pull along over any surface he rode upon. Hard-packed trail or soft deep snow didn't seem to make any difference if he didn't do anything dumb. At this point, he knew very well, if he let his concentration and powers of observation wane, the trail would bite him in some way, and make him regret his lack of focus. After his years in the bush, Caraway reacted to any situation by instinct. He had been at it so long, he didn't have to think about being careful. It was his way now.

About half way to the homestead, Denny stopped to check the fuel level. It was obvious this new rig got much better fuel mileage, the tank still holding plenty of gas. He topped it up anyway. Lifting the engine hood and checking the oil tank, he saw it had used little oil as well. He continued on his way, all the hassles of the last few days forgotten.

It was dark when Denny got home. As was his custom, he shut off the machine and sat for a while, appreciating the sudden silence, grateful to be back. The clear night sky, unhindered by artificial light, revealed vast numbers of bright stars.

Taking the headlamp out of his pack, he switched it on, the bright beam lighting his way to the cabin. As soon as he opened the door, he was dismayed by what he saw. The inside of the cabin was a complete ruin. There were cans, bags, and boxes scattered all over the floor and on the little counter. What had been on the table was on the floor too. Most of what had been in the food containers was gone, the rest spread and smeared all over the place. He smelled molasses, coffee, and other scents.

Closing the door, he lit the kerosene lantern, shut off his headlamp, and closely inspected the cabin. At first he thought a bear had somehow gotten in, but the window was okay, and the door had still been latched.

Then he saw a hole had been literally ripped open at ground level in one corner of the cabin. Insulation, tarpaper, and several inner wall boards had been torn away so roughly, it looked as though a small explosion had done the work. Denny knew what had caused it when he saw the clump of long cream-colored hairs caught on the rough edge of the hole. Wolverine.

This was the first time one of these voracious and aggressive animals had come calling, though he had seen their tracks often enough. Now, the extra days spent dealing with his recent problems came back to irritate him. Maybe if he had gotten home on time he wouldn't have to deal with this.

Denny never spent much time brooding over things. Going into his storage shed he found a piece of scrap plywood and nailed it to the outside of the cabin wall where the glutton had torn its way through. Gathering up the torn insulation, he stuffed it between the wall studs, and duct taped a piece of tarpaper over it. The cabin was whole and snug again.

Denny went out to the sled and pulled the perishables from under the tarp, taking them inside the cabin so they wouldn't freeze. After getting the wood stove going, Denny looked around, mumbled, "Damn wolverine," and began cleaning up the mess, which he had to do before bringing in the dry goods and other supplies. The next day he would stash things in their proper places. Denny found the animal had also torn off the insulated lid to the cooler box. He put the butter, bacon, cheese, and eggs in and laid the lid on top. He would fix it tomorrow too. He was glad this had happened when there was little food left.

It took a couple of hours to clean up, and Denny was weary from the long day. He was sitting quietly, having a cup of tea before unloading the supplies, when he heard a tearing sound and then a deep growl outside. Grabbing his headlamp and the .44, he yanked open the front door and flashed the beam of light where he knew the sled to be. Sure enough, there was the wolverine, standing on the heavy tarp covering the sled load of goods, tearing at it and growling. It must have known Denny was there, especially with the beam of bright light playing right on it. Still, the always ravenous animal simply kept on working at the tarp. Denny touched off a round, but aimed high, and missed his target.

When he fired, the little beast turned his head towards Caraway and snarled loudly, before jumping off the sled and scurrying into the darkness.

Frustrated, and a little surprised he had missed, Denny went inside, put on his parka, hat, and gloves again, and began unloading all the supplies, stacking them in the cabin.

It was in the wee hours of the morning by the time Denny got all the supplies safely inside. He hoped the wolverine was permanently scared off by the shot, but knew they were stubborn and tenacious creatures, and it might return. Caraway wanted to leave some bait out and wait for it to come back so he could put an end to its depredations. The cold, darkness, and his weariness vetoed that idea. Returning to the cabin, he set the stove for the night, took off his boots, lay down, and covered himself with the blankets. It only took a minute for him to fall asleep.

Denny had no idea what time it was when the loud sharp sounds of ripping wood awakened him. Retrieving the headlamp lying on the floor by his bed, he turned it on, picked up the .44 and, sitting on the side of the bed, waited. It took little time for the glutton to rip off the plywood patch. When it shoved its head through the insulation and tarpaper, Denny was ready. At such short range he couldn't miss. The sound of the shot was deafening in the small cabin, but a second one wasn't necessary. The animal had been blown back out the hole it had made, struck by the heavy bullet. Denny sat still a while, listening. There was only silence.

Pulling on his boots, he went outside, to find the wolverine dead, its head a mess. Despite the necessity of removing the troublemaker, Denny found no joy in killing it. He took an animal's life out of necessity, for food or for keeping his life intact as he had just done. He had no love for the process.

Caraway took the wolverine and placed it in the storage shed where it would freeze quickly. In a few days, he would skin it and later he would tan the hide. He wasn't a trapper, but knew what to do. He would put the carcass some distance away from the cabin to be eaten by other animals.

Exhausted, he nailed the ripped off piece of plywood back on. A permanent fix could wait. For now, he wanted only to hit the blankets for some much-needed sleep.

Chapter Eight

The remainder of the winter went by without any more adventures, of either the fun or life-threatening kind, which suited Denny just fine. He spent the days doing chores, hiking around on snowshoes, reading, eating, and sleeping, the remoteness of his home allowing him the peaceful solitude he desired. Loneliness had not been a factor for him since he had become a homesteader, not even after he moved to this more isolated area.

One project he was looking forward to was building a new cabin, a log cabin, which he planned to start in the late spring after break-up. He had already begun gathering birch logs for it. Denny still had the book on building log cabins he had purchased before coming to Alaska. It was written by a man named Walker, someone well known in Alaska for living and working in the bush as guide, builder, and photographer. The book was well written, and even though Denny had opted for a frame cabin on his first homestead, he always regretted not doing a log structure. Now, he would build one. He had the time, the tools, the trees, and the ability.

The snow machine served well for hauling logs to the building site, situated about twenty yards farther away from the creek. By winter's end he had accumulated over forty logs, which he figured was enough for building what he had planned, a sixteen-by-twenty foot cabin, with a small storage loft to be built along the last six feet of the structure. He would have a three-by-four foot window of the modern sliding type in the south wall and one more on the east side. There would be a porch at one end with a six-foot roof overhang to keep precipitation off, and he planned on building a stone fireplace into one of the sidewalls. He'd also have a small wood stove in one corner of the cabin for cooking, and extra heat in the coldest time of winter. Though Denny knew a fireplace was not as efficient for heating as a wood stove, he had a reason for wanting to build one.

Several years before, he had purchased a book about Richard Proenneke, who had lived in a very remote area near Lake Clark National Park, on the shore of Twin Lakes, Alaska. There, he built what Caraway could only call an exquisite little trappers cabin. To Denny's mind it was perfect, a work of art really. Proenneke had even fashioned a Dutch door and made the hinges from naturally-bent pieces of native spruce. The cabin had a traditional sod roof as old-time sourdoughs had used, that ended up looking more like a small meadow of grasses and wild flowers than a cabin roof. Proenneke's crowning achievement, Denny believed, was the hand-made fireplace he had designed and built. He used stones from the lake shore, including a stone lintel.

So Caraway, as a sign of admiration and respect for Mr. Proenneke's accomplishments living alone in a primitive paradise for over thirty years, would emulate him by building a similar fireplace, if not exactly in design, then certainly by intent. Denny wasn't a man easily impressed by other people, but he would, if the occasion ever arose, openly say Proenneke was high on his list.

Denny worked in the evenings by lantern light, drawing plans for his cabin, refining the small log structure to suit his way of living. Even though it would be a simple structure, there were lots of details to work out. Denny was determined to arrange the interior in as efficient a way as possible.

He had found two birch trees of medium size with large burls on the trunks. When stripped of their bark and finished with log oil, they would make dandy upright supports for the front porch. He would use some small spruce poles as a railing for the porch and the loft, mostly for cosmetic purposes. By the time spring showed up, he had a great set of plans.

Chapter Nine

Spring came early, with the first hint of break-up coming in late March, rather than April or even May. Denny needed to make a supply run for perishable foods before break-up made traveling by snow machine or ATV impossible. He had a good stock of dry goods, having learned what would be gone well before summer's end, and he would only have to go as far as the Salcha grocery store to get the small items he needed, then head home the same evening. It made for a tough round trip, but he felt better getting right back to the homestead, especially after the wolverine incident.

Caraway was glad he had the new snow machine to use on this trip. He still had the ATV he had used on the first homestead and old as it was, it ran well. He didn't use it much during the snowless season except to gather firewood, or trees for building, dragging in the logs to cut up at home. It was better to stay close to home during the spring and summer months, using the wheeler to get to the road only out of necessity.

The summer trail he used was a work in progress, a number of areas needing to be cleared for ease of travel. In stretches thick with brush and trees, Denny only widened the trail enough to ride the wheeler through. He didn't want to have a wide-open trail because it would make it easier for people to ride. He knew he had no right to keep people off. Despite the work he put in, it technically wasn't his trail; it was simply his preference to keep it as private as possible.

The weather was warming up quickly, so Denny left early in the morning when the snow was at its coldest, making for a firmer surface to ride on. He would only need to use the rear rack and the back portion of the long seat for the amount of goods he needed to buy, making the sled unnecessary. Without it to hold him back, there were several areas where he could let the machine stretch its legs. At one long flat spot he hit fifty miles an hour, faster than he could have gone with his old machine. He'd had another snow machine on the first 'stead, and even though it was fairly light and reliable, it got stuck far too easily in deep or wet snow, though Denny wasn't sure why. So he had sold it, choosing to use the old machine he had gotten from George Levine when he'd purchased the Lanyard Creek land from him.

Once he got to the road, Denny ran alongside the pavement up to the North Star Cafe. He had worked up a strong appetite on the trail. Charlie Brady made a good burger and home fries, though nothing could match Hazel O'Mara's burgers. Of course, he'd never mention that to Charlie.

When the homesteader arrived, Charlie greeted him as always, with a cup of coffee made the way Denny liked it, black with a dash of cinnamon in it, something he had gotten attached to at Hazel's cafe. Their greetings to each other were always the same.

"Afternoon, Mr. Caraway," Charlie said.

"Afternoon, Officer Brady," Denny responded.

Charlie was feeling talkative, so he asked Denny how the trip to Hazel had gone.

Denny gave a little shrug of his shoulders and said it was "Nothing to write home about, just saying goodbye to another friend. I hope I don't have to do it too often."

"I know the feeling all too well," the retired Alaska State Trooper noted, getting a far-away look in his eyes.

Denny nodded. He knew Charlie had been in the Troopers for a long time and must have seen a number of friends and acquaintances go down.

By way of changing the conversation, Charlie asked, "So, Denny, have you heard about the Alaskan environmental group that's trying to keep motorized vehicles out of wildlife refuges and state recreational areas? Probably not a snowball's chance in hell of getting a bill pushed through, as it's contrary to what most Alaskans would want, including you, I'd wager. It could affect you getting out to the homestead."

Denny gave Charlie one of his long, deep looks. Even though Brady had been through more than most people ever know about, there was something about Caraway's intense stare that made even him want to take one mental step back, though he didn't let it show.

Using Brady's first name, an unusual thing, Denny said, "Charlie, I like living a peaceful, trouble-free life, but it wouldn't make one bit of difference to me either way. If I need to come out or go in to my place, nothing would stop me from doing so."

"And you'd get no problems out of me, Denny, even if I was still on duty. Some things ought to be left as they are. I'd have your back, no matter what."

"I know you would, and I appreciate it."

That was the end of the conversation. Denny paid his tab, nodded at Charlie who responded in kind, and left to make his purchases so he could get back home again.

Charlie Brady made a mental note to himself: "Denny Caraway hasn't gone totally bushy, but he sure seems to be a little feral these days."

Caraway wasn't sure why, but he decided to stay the night at the trailer. He never questioned his gut any more, but simply went with whatever it told him. Besides, he really didn't mind not running out the trail until the next day. The bed in the trailer was comfortable and he could always listen to some music on the old record player George left behind.

Denny took some more moose stew from the refrigerator's freezer and a big piece of fry bread from his pack. It was simple fare, but tasty. He put on a recording of Tchaikovsky's Nutcracker Suite. He was pleased when he'd first gone through the record collection George had accumulated. It was a varied collection, from classic to blues to Big Band, so Denny could always find something to suit his mood the times he'd stayed in the trailer, though the Big Band sounds were not really to his taste, too loud and raucous.

Feeling restless, he browsed through the closet in the bedroom. Some of Levine's personal possessions were still there, including a photo album. Denny wondered why George had left it. Perhaps it was for Denny's sake, but he'd never know.

After his meal, Denny sat on the couch and looked through the album. A lot of the photos were typical family images. George had apparently come from Kansas, and the farm in the background of many of the shots must have been his family's property. It sure looked like a hardscrabble place. There were enough images for Caraway to see how George had grown up. Most of the photos showed him doing some kind of farm work, even as a young boy.

He began seeing more images of George, probably in his late teens in a U.S. Marines uniform, the photos dated during World War II. As he kept looking, Denny became more and more impressed with George the Marine. He had obviously been in combat in the Pacific, and some of the later photos taken after the war showed him to be in frogman gear, as a member of the UDT, as written on the back of several shots, forerunner of the Navy Seals. He'd apparently transferred over from the infantry after the war. The last photo showed an older George in uniform, with a pretty girl on his lap, beer bottle in hand, surrounded by a bunch of smiling, drunken sailors. The photo caption read, "Bon voyage, Frogman Levine. Keep your ammo dry." The date was August, 1966. He had served twenty-five years in the service, and not behind a typewriter, either.

The rest of the photos were of George in Alaska, the earliest dated 1967. They showed him hunting, fishing, panning for gold, and building a log cabin somewhere in the bush. One showed him standing in front of a small plywood cabin, which looked freshly built. Denny recognized it as the cabin he was living in on Lanyard Creek. In the photo, George was standing with his friend Mitch, the man who had introduced Caraway to George.

Denny was sorry he hadn't had time to get to know Levine better when he was still around. After going through the album, he felt he knew him a little better. He could relate to how George had matured in the military, seeing how he had changed through the war and in the years afterwards. It connected with him as to how he himself had "come of age" as a homesteader, developing into the person he had to be to survive and thrive in wild country. Though he would never compare himself to a man who had fought in combat, willing to sacrifice all for what he believed in, still there was that element to his existence. There was always the chance a deadly situation might prove his end. Denny nodded to himself. It seemed as if, even though alone and isolated on his homestead, he was still an element on the wheel of life, a part of the whole process.

Caraway put the album back in the closet and went to bed. Morning would come soon enough and he wanted to be rested for the run in.

Chapter Ten

The snow on the trail was nice and firm when Denny headed out to his cabin. By the time he was half way home, however, the air temperature had risen dramatically, above the freezing mark, and the snow had softened noticeably by the time he'd reached the homestead. Denny knew spring break-up was right around the corner.

Later that week, he heard loud cracking and grinding noises from Lanyard creek. The ice was breaking up. Though the creek was not particularly wide, its main channel had some depth, so the ice was pretty thick in the middle. Now, it was jamming up with large, jagged chunks of ice. Denny loved the whole process, the transition to spring, though it was a relatively short season this far north. He considered it simply a lead-in to summer.

His plywood cabin was located on a slight rise of land, far enough from the edge of the creek to be safe from the ice jams. The melting snow in spring drained down easily, allowing the soil around the cabin to dry quickly. George had chosen the cabin site well.

A few days later, winter was well on its way out. He could see the stacked metal roofing he had hauled in the previous winter, now freed from the covering of snow that had hidden it for months. Proenneke had made the roof of his cabin out of sod. Denny wanted to use a more durable material, forgoing the esthetic quality a sod roof would provide. He had lots of years left and knew sheet metal roofing would be a longer-lasting material to use. He opted for a dark brown color, rather than green or bare metal.

Break-up had arrived and Denny couldn't do any traveling for a few weeks, but in a week to ten days time, he could start work on his new cabin, his main project for the coming warmer months.

As he had anticipated, Denny was soon able to begin working on the cabin. He would have a wooden floor in the place, instead of a tamped-earth floor like the one in George Whiting's old cabin outside Hazel. He was in the habit of walking around in his socks, so a smooth board floor was necessary for them to survive for long. Denny had felt a little funny about wanting a hard floor for such a reason, until he realized he could do any damn thing he wanted to do, and for any reason that suited him. After all it was his life, free and clear.

The building of his cabin was a straightforward lesson in notched log construction. He liked the way notched logs looked, and was determined to do it well. Walker's book had a warning on the first page stating that a person's first attempt at log cabin building probably wouldn't be perfect. Caraway was determined to do a proper job, and when he set his mind to something, that was all there was to it.

The main thing he learned was that building with logs was heavy, time-consuming work. He had to peel the bark off the logs with a draw knife, choose the right logs to lay together for the best fit, and cut the notches as carefully as he could using a compass for scribing the right shape and size of notch for each pair of logs. Denny proved to be a natural at log construction, skillful enough to get the whole job done right.

The hardest part of the process for him was rolling the upper-level wall logs into place. These twenty and twenty-four foot logs he had picked for the same ten-inch diameter were heavy. He had cut them overlong to allow for trimming later. He was able to use the winch attached to the front end of his old wheeler to pull them up onto the walls, stopping to lock the logs in place with wooden wedges on two logs he used for a ramp, resetting the winch cable again, then pulling the logs up higher. It took three pulling sessions to get the highest wall logs into place.

While setting the next to last log on the south wall, when he had come back around to place the wedges, the winch cable end had come loose, the log had slipped free, and rolled back down the ramp, the end of the log grazing his lower leg, knocking him off his feet.

Luckily, the log had not landed on him. From then on, Denny made sure to always set the cable right. Being all alone as he was, he had to be extra cautious. There would be no help coming if he got jammed up. As it was, Denny had a sore leg for days to remind him of his moment of carelessness.

Making the loft had added some complications, but he sat down with a mug of tea and studied the log cabin building book. It described the process of putting in a second floor, setting cross poles for flooring notched into the main walls, and it was easy to adapt the process to make a sturdy loft.

Sooner than he had anticipated, he had a complete log frame waiting to be roofed.

Even though he wanted to continue working on the cabin until it was completed, Caraway had to take time out for normal chores, such as gathering, cutting, and splitting enough firewood for the year. He had to can up what meat was left from the big bull moose he had taken. It was the largest moose he had ever shot, and there was more meat left after winter than he had expected. It took all the canning jars to get the job done, and then he had plenty of ground and cut up meat to last until next season, as well as more jerky.

Before doing the roof, Denny needed to gather ten more logs to finish the roof ends and beams. The beams would be a little tricky. Because he was going to use metal roofing, he'd have to mill one flat side on each roof beam, then mill some boards to act as purlins on which to screw the metal roofing. Working slowly and methodically, he was able to set the beams correctly. Milling the boards he needed for the metal sheets was no problem. He had milled all the wood for his cabin on the first homestead, and it was second nature to him. Denny still had the same chain saw mill he had used for that first cabin. It was old and rough looking, with dried pitch all over it, but still worked fine. He had to make a guide for the first leveling and squaring cuts. That too was no problem.

Once the main structure was done, including the roof, he cut the window and the front door openings, and framed them in with more milled wood. He over-sized one of the two window openings and had to mill a new frame of thicker boards to bring the dimensions back down, and that did the trick. He chinked the wall logs with a special mixture Ed Gundross had told him about in one of their many conversations about building cabins. It was a compound made of common ingredients, which hardened into a semi-flexible sealant which would move with temperature changes instead of cracking and falling out. It was white, so it looked good between the logs.

The most milling he had to do was for the flooring. He cut vertical notches in the lowest row of the east and west wall logs to fit floor joists into, the ends of the joists notched to match the slots in the logs. After that it was simply a matter of milling and nailing down the floorboards, full-dimensioned two by eights. He had hunted for some big spruce trees to make the floor boards. It had taken several days to find them and cut short trails in to where he would fell the trees, buck them into the right lengths, then mill them into dimensional lumber, before stacking them to dry.

Caraway found he enjoyed milling more than he had when making the boards for his earlier cabin. It was a rough go, dragging them to the new cabin site, though. As usual, he didn't think about how much work it was; he just got it done. Denny used his draw knife to smooth out one side of each floorboard for walking on. It was tedious work, but every time he wearied of it, he thought how nice it would be to have a smooth floor, and continued on.

Temperatures were in the fifties by then, though bugs were not out yet. Denny worked without a shirt on most of the time, a real treat after the long hard winter. Once the mosquitoes, no-see-ums and black flies were out, he'd be wearing hard-woven shirts tightly buttoned.

The day came when he walked through the door of his completed cabin. The hand-made door of narrow milled birch boards didn't look as fancy as Proenneke's Dutch door. But Denny too had formed hinges out of wood, using metal bolts slipped into matching holes on both parts of the hinge, instead of dowels. It would do.

The only thing left was to build the fireplace. He didn't like having to cut the large opening in the wall where the fireplace would be located, but he measured repeatedly to make sure the dimensions were correct. Referring to Proenneke's book, Caraway built it of stones he hand-picked from the banks of Lanyard Creek. It took a lot of stones to have enough to get the top of the chimney several feet higher than the roof ridge. He built wooden forms of milled wood to support the stone and mortar body of the fireplace and chimney, fitting in a metal flue he had bought at a heating store in Fairbanks.

He messed up the first time, and had to break the flue out of the hardened mortar, getting it right the second time. Building the whole she-bang had taken him several weeks, and the first time he set a fire in it, he forgot to open the flue, smoking up the new cabin. When he opened the flue, it had drawn beautifully. The heavy metal stove pipe he installed on top of the chimney looked good with the conical cap he had fitted to it.

Denny moved the woodstove into the new place from the plywood cabin, positioning it at the other end of the cabin from the fireplace, cutting the hole needed to run the stove pipe out through the roof. It had been a real struggle to haul the heavy woodstove over to the cabin, but as planned, the cabin door was wide enough to let it pass through with a bit of wiggling. He used a plumb line to position the stovepipe collar on the stove body directly under the hole in the roof. He ran the stovepipe up through and made the outside of the hole watertight with some sheet metal flashing and sealant. Now he could be sure of having two heat sources in the coldest part of winter, and a good stove to cook on.

Denny Caraway's cabin was complete, and he was satisfied with the job he'd done. Because of his solitary life, he had to enjoy the experience, this good moment, by himself, as he had previously when he'd done something he was proud of.

Standing in front of his new home, he nodded in acknowledgment of his creation. Caraway called it a day and went inside his new home to enjoy a cup of Labrador tea, and a few Oreos.

It took several days to move all his possessions into the new place, leaving some of his gear in the plywood shack, which would make a good storage shed for his extra equipment and supplies.

Over the next several weeks, Denny built the interior cabinets and shelving. It was enjoyable, a real labor of love, as was building the cabin itself. Finishing the interior, Denny felt more connected to his new home, having given up lots of sweat and a little blood to construct it.

Standing by the creek bank one morning, admiring the cabin, Denny felt a deep sense of satisfaction and contentment. There was a certain joy in knowing every log and board was worked and fitted by his own hands. Acting spontaneously, he jumped into the creek, but the icy cold water instantly brought him to his senses and to dry land with a loud "WOW!" He stood there feeling foolish and happy all at once.

Sitting by the fireplace in his new home that first evening, Denny let his mind drift as he watched the open fire. He had, as was required in the early days, proved up his homestead, developed it in appropriate ways.

Despite his years of living remote, Denny often felt the same way he did the first day he had come into the Alaska bush, that pure sense of wonder and excitement. Being in this newest cabin brought back memories of how it was that first night in the cabin he had built on his land outside Hazel. The large frame structure had taken much longer to build, the hand milling, transporting, and construction taking all of five years.

Then Denny reflected on why he'd decided to leave, the hassles with his homesteading neighbor and nemesis, Bucky Waters and with Monty Leer too, being the last straw for him. Dealing with Waters at Ed's reception had settled a lot for Denny, but he'd never forget what had occurred, and it was the reason he was so determined to hold on to his new place. Hopefully, he would never have to be put to the test.

Chapter Eleven

The fourth winter Denny Caraway was on his Lanyard Creek homestead seemed a perfect time for him. It was the kind of life he had craved when he'd migrated to the Alaska wilderness. Nothing happened to disrupt his daily living. No marauding animals, or humans for that matter, no mechanical failures with his equipment, and no painful accidents. Even the winter weather was mild for the area, moderate snowfall and temperatures rarely dropping lower than ten below zero. Denny gathered his wood and food, got his clean water from the creek, ate, read, and slept well. All in all, it was a fine time.

While someone who had never lived the life might think being a homesteader had to include adventure and excitement to be complete and satisfying, well, such a person had a lot to learn, if he was able.

Denny made his two yearly supply runs to Fairbanks, one at the beginning of winter and one just before break-up, paid his visits to Charlie Brady at the North Star Cafe, got his winter moose in fall, and a small black bear for food in the spring. Life was good, and Denny was content.

The next summer, Denny was in the lean-to behind his cabin, replacing several worn hub bearings on his snow mobile's track wheels. He paused, hearing a motor and voices. Walking around to the front, he saw two men in a side-by-side ATV pulling onto his property.

The hairs on his neck stirred, something which happened when Caraway sensed potential trouble. One of the men appeared to be a field worker of some sort, a miner or oil man. The other one seemed more like a supervisor or engineer.

When they saw Caraway, they gave each other a quick glance, then shut the ATV's engine off. Walking toward him, they stopped at a slight distance, the look on Denny's face making them do so.

He said, "Come to see me, or just passing through?"

"Well," the bossy looking one said, "If this is your property, then we should talk."

"And just what would we have to talk about?" Denny already had a feeling he knew what the stranger was about to say.

"We work for Genesis Mining Corporation, and this general area is going to be part of a new project we plan to develop. It's been written up in several papers and on TV."

In the low tone Denny spoke in when he was getting or was already bothered by something, he responded. "Does it look to you like I get a paper delivered, or have an antenna to get television reception?"

A sheepish grin on his face, the bossy guy told Denny he "did have a point there."

"So, what is it you want to tell me?"

"Well, uh, what did you say your name was?"

"I didn't; it's Caraway."

"Well, Mr. Canary,"

"I said Caraway, C-a-r-a-w-a-y."

"Right, Caraway. Well, this stretch of Creek #27 is going to be fully developed all the way up to the hills over there to the south. There's an old mine up in there, hasn't been worked since the late forties. You might have seen it? It's actually the center of the mine site we're going to work."

"Has this project already been approved by the state?" Denny asked, his patience and tolerance for undesired company wearing thin.

"Oh, not quite yet, lots of formalities to go through. It's going to bring lots of revenue to the area, and jobs for the locals."

"I suppose my land will be a part of this project of yours?"

Something about the way Denny spoke made the bossy guy pause in his spiel. "Uh, it will be right in the heart of things. I'm sure someone will come talk to you about an offer on your place, if it comes to that."

"Since you have the right to pass by my place if you're taking the trail farther in, I suggest you do just that, now. Our conversation is over."

The bossy guy got red in the face, probably not used to being spoken to like that. "There's no need to be unfriendly, you know."

"Oh, really. You come onto my land and tell me you're planning on turning it into the bottom of a tailings pile, and probably screw up the creek in the process, and I have no reason to be rude. Well, let me put it another way: get the hell off my place, now!"

The field worker, who had stood quietly until then, took a step forward, a serious look on his face.

"I wouldn't," Denny said, his voice low and steady.

The guy paused in his steps towards Caraway, sensing he might not want to start something after all.

"Forget it," said the other man. "Let's go." He held out a business card to Caraway, who made no move to take it, and let it drop to the ground. The two men got into the ATV, turned around, and headed back the way they had come.

Denny stood there a while, bad feelings stirring around in his mind and gut. The situation had brought back the reason he had left his first homestead. He had sworn to himself he would never be forced to leave his home again. He hoped it would never come to that, but there seemed there was a chance it might.

Denny went inside the lean-to and finished replacing the bearings, then went into the cabin and poured a cup of coffee from the pot keeping warm on the wood stove. He tried to settle down, his mind still filled with unpleasant thoughts. Several times during the summer, Denny heard mechanical noises in the distance coming from the far side of Lanyard Creek, and once saw a chopper fly over pretty low. The goings on concerned and irritated him, but there was nothing he could do.

Denny needn't have worried. It turned out the project was going to cost far more than it would yield, and the whole plan was scrapped. Caraway's forest sanctuary was still safe. Denny learned of the cancelled project from Charlie Brady at the cafe, and was glad of it.

Fall came and Denny took his moose, finished gathering enough wood for winter, and generally made things shipshape on the 'stead. He hadn't heard any foreign noises in the woods for quite a while, and his run-in with the mining people faded away.

Chapter Twelve

Near the end of the next December, the weather warmed to ten above zero. There had been over two feet of snowfall already, during several weeks of extremely low temperatures that came earlier than usual. Denny felt as if spring had come back, the change in temperature was so great. He knew winter was far from over, and savored the warming.

With his stock of wood in good shape, and plenty of meat and other foods on hand, he decided he could take a couple of days to explore an area nearby he hadn't headed into before and was curious about. It was a range of hills to the southeast, across Lanyard Creek. This felt like a good time to satisfy his curiosity.

Denny had his gear and supplies for a short snowshoeing trip ready and waiting. Anticipating spending a night under the trees, he had a small tarp for making a shelter, and would spread a ground covering of spruce boughs for insulation against the snow. He used his light, warm down sleeping bag, attaching it beneath a small pack containing basic emergency essentials and quick foods such as moose jerky, fry bread, and a home-made trail mix from bulk foods he had purchased in Anchorage. He had a small metal can with a wire loop handle for boiling water, a baggie of instant coffee, and one of Labrador tea. He could also boil some of the jerky for a tasty hot broth. He brought along several whips of licorice as well. He would take his .44, leaving the old Winchester 30-06 at home, not expecting anything his revolver couldn't handle.

The long darkness of winter would normally be a drawback to a long hike, but the full moon now dominating the night sky would make travel not only easier, it also added to the enjoyment, the eeriness of exploring by moonlight providing a little extra excitement. Denny didn't play by the rules most hikers and campers did. He was a capable and accomplished woodsman, and he followed his own mind when it came to being in the woods.

The next morning, Caraway headed out on his sojourn into new territory. The snow was settled, making for good snowshoeing. Denny could travel by snowshoe with ease now, not like those first few attempts years ago, when his inexperience had him coming back covered with snow from the falls he had taken while learning the basic north country skill. Now, he could set a mile-eating pace for hours. The bright moonlight in a clear sky enabled him to easily find his way.

He was about three miles from his homestead, having crossed Lanyard Creek and hiked along the flat wooded country on the other side, crossing another, smaller stream before he reached the hills beyond, which had drawn him into this new area. There was some actual daylight now, though it wouldn't last long this late in the season. Standing and scanning the slopes ahead of him, he was pleased to see the hillsides were not particularly steep, so Denny kept his snowshoes on and started up the hill directly in front of him. The trees growing up the slope were not too dense, which made for easier travel too.

After hiking uphill for half an hour he came to a wide level area, looking as if it had been bull-dozed into the hillside. He moved along the flat, which was about fifty yards wide and almost as deep. About half-way across, he saw what looked to be a small depression in the hillside. When he moved closer, it appeared to be a cave opening. His curiosity piqued, he took off his snowshoes, and used one to dig away the snow partially filling the gap in the hillside. There was no frost around the opening, so he knew there was no big, warm animal bedded down inside.

It didn't take long to discover it was actually a man-made opening. There was enough light to see there were some wooden beams about ten feet inside the opening, one on each side and one along the top held up by the other two. It was an old mine, and Denny thought it might be the mine those two unwanted visitors had mentioned last summer.

In the reading he had done on the area, he had learned there had been some mining around the turn of the twentieth century and some in the nineteen thirties and forties, but had seen no sign of it along the main trail to his homestead or the general area around it, which he had already explored. He thought about entering the mine for a little exploration, then decided to come back later and use it as a shelter for the night.

Back on snowshoes, he skirted around the mine site and continued up the slope. It took another half-hour to reach the top. The view from there was spectacular, the forests and rivers beyond offering a wonderful panorama. Denny drew a deep breath at the sight. He had a great love and admiration for Alaska and its incredible territory, which began as soon as he'd come into the state. Even though he had done a lot of research before he had originally traveled north, nothing could have prepared him for the reality of it all. Now, he couldn't conceive of living anywhere else. He planned on living his entire life here, deep in the bush, no matter how long that might be or whatever happened. Views such as this refreshed his enthusiasm.

Denny moved along the hilltop at a steady pace, intent on walking to its end to see what was there, after which he would head back to the mine to enjoy the shelter it would provide for the night.

He had gone about a half mile along the hill when he came to the edge of a steep slope, which descended to a creek far below. Caraway wasn't sure if it was Lanyard Creek farther downstream than he had been before, or another branch of the Salcha River. He stood considering things and observing the area below him for several minutes when he suddenly knew he was no longer alone. Someone or something was behind him.

Denny slowly drew his .44 and turned around. What he saw was a large grizzly bear on all fours, staring intensely at him. He saw in the brief moment they looked at each other that it was an old bear, too gaunt to be likely to survive its long winter sleep. It was certainly out looking for food. The poor, rubbed coat of fur and boney appearance somehow added to the ominous stance it had taken. He wondered if this starving animal had followed his snowshoe trail, or merely happened on him by chance. Whatever the case, this was just plain bad.

The bear's ears laid back, he lifted slightly off his front feet and leapt towards Denny, amazingly fast in spite of its haggard condition, desperation driving it forward. Denny got off one quick shot before the bear was on him. Charged with adrenaline and the desire to survive, he managed to turn away as the bear struck at him with its massive right paw, its three-inch claws flashing in the air as they ripped across Denny's left arm.

The force of the strike knocked Denny down the slope, and he rolled, bounced, and tumbled down its steep face. The action of the fall caused the snow behind him to come sliding down. It wasn't really an avalanche, but enough came down to bury him when he came to a stop near the base.

Denny had lost consciousness, having thumped his head on something under the snow. He'd lost a snowshoe, but his pack was still holding by one strap. Somehow, he had held onto the .44, which was now thoroughly packed with snow.

Denny came around, unsure of how long he had been out. Lying still, not wanting to move quite yet, he studied his situation, and found he wasn't buried too deeply, as the slight amount of fading light coming through the snow told him. His head hurt, but moving his left hand up to the sore spot, he couldn't feel any blood. Moving his left arm higher over his head, Denny experienced sharp burning pain, but by moving his arm back and forth, was able to break through the covering of snow. Widening the opening, Denny listened to learn if the bear had followed him down, but heard nothing. He wasn't sure how long he had been lying there. If it was still alive, the bear would have found him easily.

The shot he had made could have been fatal, but he wouldn't know until he had dug his way out. Carefully moving his right arm, the pistol tightly held in his right hand, caused no pain. He continued to push the snow away from up above his head until he could clearly see the sky, and then began wiggling around, kicking his legs as though swimming, finally working his way out, the one remaining snowshoe coming off his foot in the process.

With his head and shoulders above the snow, Denny looked around. Far up the slope just below the top, lay the bear, its head and one foreleg stretched out in front of him. He had apparently died right after whacking Denny. Caraway knew it could have gone very differently. Letting go of what might have been, Denny concentrated on his present situation. All the way out now, he saw three claws had racked his upper left arm through the parka, penetrating to his flesh. He knew the gouges were deep, yet the blood flow that surely would have come seemed to have ceased. Perhaps lying in the cold snow had slowed down the bleeding.

Looking at the pistol, he put it back in the holster after clearing out the packed snow as much as possible.

In spite of his predicament, he was reminded of the slough he had slipped and fallen into years before, losing his pistol, when he had hiked in to locate his first homestead site. He had almost given up and turned back, but continued on instead, the better for it. He'd retrieved his pistol from the channel of muddy water and had to clear out grit and mud to make it capable of firing, before continuing on. This time, he'd be unsure if the pistol would work if needed, unable to clear all the packed snow still clogging its action. He knew he could do little to fully clear it until he got back to the cabin.

Back to the cabin, now there was a sweet thought. Denny decided the best and easiest thing to do was move down to the bottom of the slope and the creek below. Slipping the pack onto both shoulders, he set out.

It didn't take long to get down to the creek. He had moved carefully down to the bottom of the slope, not wanting to set off another snow slide. Upon reaching the hard-frozen creek, he'd follow it as long as it went in the right general direction. The relatively light layer of snow on the creek's surface was easy enough to walk on. His wounds had begun bleeding however, and the pain was working on him, drawing away his energy. Taking the holster off its belt and tucking it into his waistband under the torn and bloody parka, he buckled the belt at the first hole, slipped the belt over his head, and used it as a makeshift sling to take the pressure off the injured arm. Taking the gun and holster in his right hand he started up the creek. He was grateful for the full moon to help him see the way.

He had hiked about a mile and a half when he met the trail his snowshoes had made on his outbound journey. It was a relief to see his own prints. The creek he had been following wasn't Lanyard after all, but the secondary, smaller stream he had crossed on his way out to the hills beyond Lanyard. Turning right, he followed the tracks to the cabin, crossing back over Lanyard in the process. The deeper snow made the walk without snowshoes exhausting for him, and though his arm was hurting badly, throbbing and aching, he held on and made it home.

Denny felt pure joy seeing the snug log cabin standing before him. He got the stove going quickly and sat close to it, waiting for the interior to warm up, and the deep cold to leave his body.

The events of the day had worn him down, and his strength was at low ebb. Leaning over in his chair, he opened his pack, pulled out a piece of jerky, and sat chewing it as the cabin slowly gained a comfortable temperature.

Denny slipped his arm out of its improvised sling and carefully unzipped the parka and removed it, grunting with the renewed pain. Taking off his flannel shirt, he inspected the wounds. They were deep, though none of the muscles seemed to be completely torn through. He knew what he had to do, and wasn't looking forward to the task. Two of the wounds definitely needed stitching. The third simply needed tight bandaging. Caraway had no other recourse than to make his own repairs.

First, he had to clean the lacerations. He went over to the little cabinet on the wall and took out the bottle of hydrogen peroxide stored there among other first aid supplies. He tore a piece of clean cloth from an unused muslin game bag, soaked it, and gently washed out the wounds. He grunted and growled as he applied the peroxide, but kept at it until it was done. Unscrewing the cap on the bottle of iodine, he soaked another piece of cloth and applied it to the wounds. Denny let out a yell as the iodine took effect. He sat there breathing quickly until the pain had subsided. Then he took out his little leather-working kit and removed the smaller of two curved needles. He found his sewing supplies, and removed a spool of heavy thread. He poured some bourbon into a small bowl and placed the needle and thread in it. He took a good swallow before putting the cap back on.

Denny took some of the now boiling water from the tea kettle and made a cup of Labrador tea. He sat there putting his thoughts away from what needed to be done next. Finishing the cup of tea, he got busy.

After threading the needle, without hesitation he put half a dozen crude stitches in the deepest wound, then five into the next. His first aid supplies provided some antiseptic ointment and bandaging material. Finally, the job done, Denny put several good-sized pieces of split wood into the stove, and lay down on his bed. He had no appetite, and in moments had dropped into a deep sleep. Just before he awoke, he had an unusual dream.

The night before he had left Nevada to come to Alaska, he'd had a dream about standing on a high bluff with his grandfather, viewing an amazing land full of rivers, lakes and mountains. Denny knew now it had been a condensed vision of Alaska. His grandfather, who had been his best friend, told him things would be fine if Caraway used what the Good Lord had given him to deal with the things to come in his life.

In the new dream, his grandfather was standing over Denny's bed there in the cabin. He was smiling, and said, "I'm proud of you, Denny. You have become the man you've always really been, and no matter what, things will come out right. I'm still watching over you."

He smiled, thanked his grandfather and got up to stoke the fire. Even though his arm was stiff and sore, he felt much better. Taking off the bandages, he saw no sign of infection. Putting on new bandages, he made a sling from more cotton muslin, and spent the day doing as little as possible — reading, drinking, eating, and napping. He would heal quickly and get on with his life soon enough.

Two weeks later, the winter bear incident was fading from his mind. His arm had healed well. Denny dressed for a trail ride, and after making sure the snow machine has enough gas and oil, strapped his emergency pack in the back rack, belted the clean, oiled .44 around his waist and rode out, following the path he had taken when he returned from the slope he had tumbled down after the attack. It didn't take long to get there this time, on his machine. Denny could see the disturbed snow where he had been buried. Hiking up to the spot, he took the little folding shovel he used on the trail and began digging. It took only a few minutes to find one of the snowshoes, but it was a while before he located the other one, the first he had lost. Luckily, he spotted a tiny bit of the tail end poking out above the snow's surface. Looking up towards the top of the slope, he didn't see the bear anymore. Undoubtedly, the predators that remained awake during the winter had made short work of the old fellow. Having found what he came for, Caraway enjoyed the ride home.

Chapter Thirteen

Late the next spring, Denny made a decision he knew would someday be necessary. He had to find work to supplement his dwindling reserves of cash.

Before leaving Nevada in 1990, he had liquefied all assets, selling his home, and cashing in his company stocks and 401K. This amounted to a substantial sum, allowing Denny to spend five years living on his first homestead without working, and be able to buy whatever he needed. He was also able to spend years on his new place in the same manner. Now, however, to keep a cash reserve for emergencies or necessary equipment he had to find work.

So, during the first week of June, Denny brought out his ATV from where it had been stored in the lean-to behind the old plywood cabin, checked it over completely, bungeed his pack and a few other things on the rear rack including his small chain saw, bar oil, and a one-gallon can of gas, in case some trail cutting was needed. He also put all perishable food in a plastic bin on the front rack, expecting to find work and not return to his homestead for quite a while. Before leaving, he screwed nail-studded bear boards over the two windows and the door of his cabin.

Having no choice, knowing anything could happen when a cabin was left on its own, Denny bit the bullet and, warming up the wheeler, headed out on the long trail leading to the Richardson Highway.

Denny had cleared the summer trail enough that it was relatively smooth to travel on. There was one area that had needed some real work. There was a creek running between two small hills, cutting across the trail as it flowed towards the Salcha. Denny had forded the creek safely the few times he had ridden the trail in summer. The last time he did, however, the creek was running high at the end of spring break-up, and his wheeler was pushed sideways in the current. He had a real struggle to get to the other bank.

So, he had built a rudimentary bridge across the creek in late summer, when the water was at its lowest. It was crude, yet sturdy. Two long birch poles ran across the creek bed, each set near its middle on a pile of large rocks, keeping the bridge well above the water except when spring break-up had it flowing hard and high. Those main poles had been a real hassle to get into position. Denny had to search the area for two suitable trees. He found and cut them down. Over twenty-five feet long and green, their weight was considerable. He lashed the birches one at a time to the back rack of his wheeler to move them to the creek.

Transporting the second pole, he hadn't tied the end tight enough to the rack, the line slipped, and the log had dropped down. When Denny ran over a hummock, the front end of the pole dug in and the wheeler had literally pivoted backwards and flipped over, slamming Denny onto his back on the ground, jammed up against the birch log. Luckily, he had been able to extend both his legs straight up, keeping the upside-down machine from falling flat on him. He finally managed to roll the ATV over sideways. He wasn't badly hurt, and was able to get the machine upright again. Still, he ached for the rest of the day. Making sure he had the pole properly tied to the rack, he continued on.

He ran the wheeler out into the creek off to one side of the pile of rocks he had built up as a middle support, stopping when the end of the pole was solidly on the other bank. Untying it from the wheeler, he had used all his strength to lift and bring the pole over the top of the rock pile, dropping it down onto it. The first pole took a set right where he wanted it to, but the second one had required extra effort to get it properly aligned and stable. As usual, Denny got it done. The poles ended up parallel with each other and surprisingly level.

He secured the pole ends in tightly with long wooden stakes driven deep into the banks on either side of the logs, using long spikes driven crosswise through the wooden stakes and the pole ends, locking them together. This would secure the bridge at times of high water, or at least Denny hoped so. Caraway was done for the day.

Over two long days, he felled more birch, rough-cutting slabs with a chainsaw to use for the bridge's riding surface. He had gotten good with his chainsaws, though he didn't like using them, never had. He didn't care for the noise and the potential danger involved. So, for years he had worked against his dislike of them, felling enough trees for firewood every year and milling scads of boards for building.

When Denny finished cutting and nailing down the slabs onto the poles, he had a sturdy, reliable bridge to traverse the stream, and it made crossing over the creek on his trip to find work a simple proposition.

As had happened during his solitary life, the homesteader momentarily longed to share the satisfaction over his accomplishment, but he only had the forest as a mute witness.

It took almost seven hours for Denny to get to the road over the trail in summer, longer by several hours than in the winter, if the snow was good. The ride was rougher too, since Denny cut as few roots as necessary where the trail went through a heavily forested area, to keep the trees alive, not simply for love of the woods, but to lessen the chance of a tree dying and falling across the trail.

It felt strange to run along the side of the paved road, once he reached it, a smooth, flat surface being alien to life in the bush. Pulling into the driveway of his mobile home, Denny shut off the engine and just sat, enjoying the sudden silence, glad to be at his destination. It was then he noticed the trailer door was open, and heard music softly playing. He knew who it was. Walking in, he found his elderly neighbor, Elliot, sitting on the couch, enjoying the classical music coming from the record player. He stood watching the old man who was lost in reverie, his eyes closed, head moving to the music. Denny quietly waited for the recording to be over.

Elliot had come up to Alaska, as many had, after World War Two. He had needed something to clear his mind and heart from all the death and misery he had witnessed in Europe. On a whim, he had decided to head north for the adventure and distraction it might provide him. Arriving in early 1946, it was love at first sight, and he had never left. He had pretty much seen it all, had "seen 'em rut," as George Levine had once told Denny. Elliot and George had met in Alaska, searched for gold, trapped, and fished together, finally settling down as neighbors where, years later, Denny had made their acquaintance.

After Elliot opened his eyes, it took him a moment to come back from wherever the music had taken him. Then he saw Caraway.

"Well, hello Denny, I'm surprised to see you here this time of year. What's up?"

"Hello, Elliot. I have to find some work to keep myself whole. Figured I might as well start looking in good weather. How are you doing?"

"Oh, you know, aches, pains and all the other joys of old age. At least I'm still here to complain. I just finished dusting the place out. It gave me something to do. Everything is good here. I started up your truck a couple of days ago, and drove it about ten miles up the road and back again. It's running good. Where are you going to look for work, Fairbanks?"

"Yeah, thought I'd go up to the Fish and Game office and see if they have anything available not requiring a degree."

"Well, I wish you luck, young man, I truly do."

"Listen, Elliot," Denny said, "I have a bunch of food I brought from the cabin, some butter, bacon and such. I was hoping you could use it."

"I sure could." Kidding, Elliot asked, "Have any unbroken eggs?"

Denny gave the faint twitch of his lip that usually passed for a smile, and said, "Oh, I might, and you could always make a big omelet if I didn't pack them right."

Denny carried the plastic bin over to Elliot's little house, telling him to leave it at the trailer when he had emptied it.

The next morning, Denny drove his truck up to Fairbanks to seek employment, hopefully in some position not requiring much close contact with people. Denny had been alone so long, any group of people made him ill at ease. Charlie Brady was right, he had become somewhat feral, most of the facades people put up in society having sloughed off during his years in the bush. Still, he needed money to do what he had to do.

The woodsman felt uncomfortable in the clean clothes he chose from the few garments he had hanging in the bedroom closet of the trailer. They felt alien to him, compared to his usual garments, torn and repaired, turned soft and comfortable through steady use and washings in creek water.

He didn't particularly enjoy the run up to Fairbanks. It was nice country to drive through, but there were some bad, deep wrinkles in the road surface from frost heaving over the winter. Some of them were so rough, the highway department would put warning signs up until they could repair them, occasionally missing some, not marking them with the usual little flagged poles, leaving drivers unaware until it was too late.

The first time he made a run up to Fairbanks, Denny had hit one of the unmarked bad ones. His heavy truck had slammed into it, then bounced higher than he would have believed possible, all four wheels leaving the ground. His head had slammed into the roof of the cab when the truck came back down and bounced, and though the homesteader had almost lost control, he managed to keep it on the road. He had pulled over and stepped out onto the side of the road, standing for a few minutes, until his adrenaline had subsided, muttering under his breath about lousy roads and non-existent work crews. After checking over the truck, especially underneath, he continued on at a reduced speed, focusing intently on the road surface.

In Fairbanks, Denny pulled over to a gas station, filled up, and asked directions to the Fish and Game office. It turned out to be only a few blocks away.

Denny stood in front of the door, steeling himself for the interactions to come. Entering, he asked the woman at the counter who to talk to about a job.

With a flat voice she told him to check the memo boards to his right. Denny looked and didn't see anything he was qualified to do. Besides, a resume and a written test was required for all of the positions, and it would mean him having to come back up to Fairbanks several more times. A notice would be mailed to him. Mailed? This wasn't going to work out. Denny knew a resume which showed he hadn't worked for the past ten years wasn't going to impress anybody.

Figuring he'd have the same hassle at the Parks Department office, Denny had to rethink his situation.

Sitting in his truck sipping a cup of fast food coffee from a foam cup, Denny considered what his next move should be. He didn't plan on working at some store in town. In fact, he knew he couldn't handle that for long, no matter how much he needed some extra cash. He was at a loss.

While he pondered his situation, he saw a sign over a store front across the street which declared "O'Bannion's Guide Service, Moose, Bear, and Caribou." Though he had never done any guiding, with all his experience living in the bush, it sounded promising to him.

Walking through the front door, he saw three men sitting together talking and laughing. They turned in unison when he walked in.

One of the men, with a bushy red beard, stood up and asked Denny what he could do for him. When Denny said he was looking for work, the man stood silent for a moment, looking at Caraway, then asked him if he had ever done any basic construction. Denny told the man he had been a homesteader for ten years and had built a large frame cabin, and a log cabin with a loft. He said, "They're both well built and solid."

Thinking a moment, the man asked Denny, "Do you hunt and have you always been successful at hunting?"

Denny thought a moment, then answered, "Yes, no, and anyone who says they have is probably lying."

The bearded man smiled, stuck out his hand and said his name was Carlton O'Bannion and "when can you start?"

"Whenever you need me," said Denny.

O'Bannion told Denny he needed to have simple cabins built in two of his camps in Hunting Unit Twenty, and did Denny know where that is?

He did.

"If you're willing to build the cabins for me, you're hired. Any problems with working under the table? I'll pay fair wages for the work, plus food."

Well, this seemed an ideal set-up to Caraway, almost as good as home-steading, only with pay. So, he nodded, and the deal was sealed with a handshake. Denny was pleased at what he felt was a perfect way for him to earn money.

Chapter Fourteen

Three days later, Denny was flying in a float-equipped Cessna 180 over some beautiful tundra and willow country southwest of Fairbanks in Game Management Unit 20A. The light aircraft landed on a small lake beside a low hill. After unloading Caraway's personal gear and other supplies, the pilot headed into the wind and was gone in minutes.

The hunting camp was on the other side of the hill just below its top on a wide bench, sheltered from the prevailing winds. There was a forested area half a mile away to the south, wide and deep. To the north spread a broad expanse of tundra running up to a range of high hills about three miles away. It was a beautiful panorama of Alaska wilderness, and Denny stood there, absorbing the perfection of this country that seemed so familiar to him. Though far from his homestead, Caraway had no doubts he could roam this country and feel right at home, having lived in the bush so long.

The first thing he did was to erect the canvas hunting tent. This tent was what clients had previously stayed in while hunting with O'Bannion. There was a low wooden platform — a floor for the tent, located on the wide, flat bench of ground just below the top of the low hill. The wooden framework for the canvas shelter was stashed under the platform, along with a metal cook stove. It took Denny a few minutes to figure the frame out, but he soon had it erected, using the bolts and wing nuts provided to hold all the pieces of lumber together. It was easy to hang the tent over the framing, taking out any slack with hold-down cords attached to the tent, using metal stakes already driven into the ground. Once Denny had the sheet metal shepherd's stove set up in the tent, and unfolded the cot brought in on the plane, he had a cozy place to sleep in, out of the elements. Denny stowed his firearms and pack at the head of the cot. He had brought his outdoor gear with him — rain suit, rifle, and pistol of course, knives, two changes of clothes, and other small but essential items.

He felt settled now, ready to work. O'Bannion had asked him if he wanted someone to help with the building, but Denny said he worked better and faster alone. Carlton took him at his word.

All the building materials needed had been provided, brought in previously by helicopter and stacked under a large plastic tarp — lumber, roofing materials, two windows, and one door. Denny located boxes of nails and screws and a large tool box containing everything he would need, including a small chainsaw and accessories for cutting the wood. O'Bannion asked Caraway if he needed a small generator and a skill saw. But the homesteader told him a good small chainsaw and sharpening tools would be fine. It seemed O'Bannion was a serious man, supplying exactly what Denny had asked for. It must have taken a number of chopper flights to bring in all the goods.

The next chore Denny had was to gather firewood for the stove. He took up the chainsaw, tested the sharpness and tension of the cutting chain, made sure the gas and oil reservoirs were full, and walked down to a nearby copse of spruce. It only took a few minutes to spot several dead dry spruces standing bare of bark and most of their branches.

In a short time, Denny had cut down the dead trees and removed all the stubs and remaining branches from the trunks. Cutting the logs into four-foot lengths, he could easily carry two at a time up to the campsite, the wood being dry and light. In an hour, Denny had a nice pile of firewood next to the tent, having cut the trunks into twelve inch lengths, splitting them with the camp axe from the tool chest.

Caraway never went anywhere without either his .44 magnum pistol or the old Winchester rifle he had used all the years he had been homesteading, the one George Whiting had given him when Denny had bought his old homestead. The rifle was old, though well cared for when he had received it, the wooden stock's finish worn down in places and the bluing rubbed off much of the metal. It had never let him down. The pistol, which he had held onto during the winter bear attack several years prior, showed signs of steady use too, the wooden grip panels scratched, chipped and dull, its bluing also worn, yet it too was still reliable. Denny figured it best to bring both guns on this project.

The one concern Denny had was to keep food out of the tent. There were plenty of interior grizzlies in this country, and he didn't want to bring them in to where he would be sleeping. So, he gathered some stones from the lake behind the hill and made a fire ring about fifty feet from the tent. He made a little fly from a plastic tarp he had brought, to block any wind. Now he had a comfortable camp to work from.

The long hours of summer daylight was great for getting work done, but made it harder to sleep, though if Denny put in a full day's work, he usually had no trouble dozing off. Still, being here in this open country without a solid shelter, his senses on general alert for any unwanted visitors, he probably wouldn't sleep as soundly as he might in his own cabin.

Denny had fried spam and canned peas for dinner along with several slices of bread and butter. Though it was summer, it would be chilly at night, so Denny kept his perishables in the shade under his cook fly in a metal box O'Bannion had provided, supposedly bear proof. Denny had smiled on seeing the food container, because the can was small and light enough that a grizz could swat it far from the camp before losing interest. Still, it was better than leaving an open buffet for the bruins in the area.

Denny tied small plastic bottles up, one at the front and one at the back of the tent, and several hanging from the tarp of the cooking area. He had made them up in Fairbanks. The eight-ounce plastic bottles were full of ammonia. A curious bear would get quite a surprise after biting into one of these, the ammonia wreaking havoc on the animal's sensitive nose, as well as tasting horrible. To entice any curious bears to the bottles, Denny had rubbed a little peanut butter on them.

Next morning was heavily overcast. Denny walked over to cabin site at the base of the little hill, where O'Bannion had put four corner stakes and began placing a stake and string system for positioning and squaring up a post foundation for the twelve-by-sixteen cabin. Though Denny had only built one frame cabin, it had been much larger and more complicated than this simple hunting shack would be.

The corners and post positions squared and lined up, he began the one chore he had never liked, digging holes, for the foundation posts. It was necessary, though, and Denny did what had to be done. Knowing the sooner he began digging, the sooner it would be over, Denny took shovel in hand. Luckily, the ground was quite soft, with few cobbles to make digging difficult, and he had the twelve holes dug fairly quickly. He cut the six-by-six posts into three-foot lengths, and set them in the ground, packing them in tightly. The twelve-by-sixteen foot platform itself went easily enough, support beams and joists, then he began nailing down the floor boards themselves.

Denny was glad to be using commercial lumber for this project. He had hand milled enough boards to last him a lifetime. It was no fun, just necessary, and it had been a good learning experience. For his own structures, however, he liked home-made boards better than the ones from the lumber yard. They just seemed "right."

Taking a break, he made a spam sandwich and a cup of instant coffee, sitting on the edge of the platform, admiring the view from his vantage point on the hillside. A few minutes into his lunch, a camp robber came flying in, neatly dressed in his gray and white outfit. He landed on the ground in front of Denny's feet, strutting back and forth like a little feathered soldier, waiting, quite obviously, for his share of food. Denny broke off a piece of the bread and spam and tossed it to the impatient bird. It jumped away a few inches at the toss, then quickly homed in on the tidbit, grabbing it in its beak, and flying away to the nearest tree. Denny knew he'd now have the gray jay for company all the while he was there. Some things never changed.

Denny recalled the raucous Stellar jays that showed up at his original homestead the first day he'd arrived. Old George Whiting had put a bird feeding platform right next to the front door of the little log cabin Denny occupied while building his new, larger cabin. The jay had no problem making his demands known and its smaller mate was willing to join in the complaining. When Denny moved up to his new cabin, the jays came right along, following their meal ticket.

Caraway realized he hadn't had any hungry birds come to his cabin on Lanyard Creek, and wondered why. When he got home, he'd put up a feeder to see if it might bring some in.

While he was considering this little enigma, rain began coming down, lightly at first, then turning into a real downpour. He trotted over to the tent to sit in his little folding chair and watch as what seemed to be a cloudburst came pouring down. He was grateful for the dry tent. Caraway was going to put some shavings and small kindling in the stove to make a fire warm up the tent when, as suddenly as it had started, the rain quit. A few minutes later, the sun came out. Walking back outside, he took a deep breath of the fragrant air, full of the smell of vegetation wetted by the rain, thinking how cleansing the rain was, then went back to work.

By the end of the day, Denny had all the floorboards nailed in place, and decided it was a good time to stop. Putting the tools away, he went down the back side of the hill, and, after looking around for any wildlife in the area, took off his shirt and washed away the sweat and sawdust in the chill water of the lake, feeling completely refreshed afterwards. If anyone was there with him, they would have seen a man with no extra weight at all, lean and hard from years of homesteading. They would also have noticed the three ragged scars running across his upper left arm, mute witnesses to the dangers of remote living.

Wiping himself dry back at the tent, he went to the cook fly, made a fire, and fixed himself a dinner of bacon and cheese sandwiches and canned bean soup. It tasted great, eaten after a good day of work in such beautiful surroundings. The gray jay came flying down just as he'd finished. There was a little piece of bacon left in the skillet. He picked it up and held it out to the bird, not expecting it to trust him. Surprisingly, the bird flew up without hesitation and landed on his wrist, looking him in the eye briefly, before grabbing at the little bit of bacon and flying away. Denny smiled, enjoying the little moment of contact. He reserved real smiles for when he was alone in the bush, barely showing one when he was around people. Denny decided this jay was used to people from hunting trips to this site.

Reaching into his pack, Caraway pulled out a brand new pipe and a pouch of pipe tobacco along with some matches. Sitting in the folding chair by the tent opening, he wet his finger and dampened the inside of the bowl as the clerk at the store had instructed him, packed the pipe with tobacco, not too tightly, then gently lit it until the bowlful was steadily burning. Leaning back, Denny puffed slowly on the stem, enjoying the taste. On a whim, he had bought the pipe and tobacco to try it out. As he smoked his first bowlful, Caraway had a feeling this was something which would stay with him.

Denny felt good. Finding work had been easier than expected, and here he was, in a part of Alaska he had never been before. Denny realized he needed this too. He was content, living on his own remote parcel of land, but being far afield in the wilderness made him feel free. At that moment, Caraway was sorry he would be alone in this open country only until the building was done. He now understood an old gem of wisdom; when you are free within yourself, then you are truly free anywhere you might be.

As if on cue, a huge bull moose walked across his line of sight, barely one hundred yards away, through some willows. He moved with strength, in his prime, knowing there was nothing he couldn't handle here in his own domain. Denny knew exactly how the moose felt. Tapping out his pipe, he went back into the tent, closed the flap and bedded down for the night.

The next several days were clear and warm, and the slight steady breeze which had been blowing since he'd arrived had stopped. The bugs would not get thick for at least several weeks, though the ones already out looking for blood were a constant reminder of what was to come. Denny was ready with bug netting and repellent. He hoped to be done here before they got bad. Even with anti-bug supplies, they could still be maddening with their buzzing and ability to slip in anywhere there was a tiny opening. He pitied the caribou and other animals in the bush, defenseless against the hordes of tiny flying monsters.

In two days' time, Denny had put up all the walls and most of the roof framing, the long daylight hours allowing him to do so. The morning of the third day was heavy with clouds, and Denny hurried to get the roof covered before the next rain storm cut loose. He'd almost finished when big drops began hitting the roof boards and him. He managed to get a tarp over the unfinished area before the skies really opened up. Putting the tools under cover and trotting over to the tent, Denny stood inside, watching the water come down, his work suspended for the time being.

Starting a fire in the sheepherder's stove, Denny made himself some Labrador tea and sat watching the rain. There wasn't much else to do. He hoped it would let up by afternoon so he could get back to work by the next morning when the roof had dried enough to make it okay to finish it. It didn't let up, however, not for the rest of that day or the next.

Two mornings later, it had slowed to a drizzle, but everything was soaked. Donning his raingear, Denny walked over to the partially-completed cabin. At least he could put up tar paper on the walls to keep some of the wet out. Though it was unpleasant, chilling work, he got enough done to keep the inside of the cabin framing reasonably protected. Denny put the two windows in place next. The door would have to wait. The roof boards had swelled enough to seal themselves from any major leaks. Satisfied he had done something, Caraway called it a day.

Trying to start a fire in the fire pit was a dismal failure, because the wood, along with everything else, was completely wet. So he had to cook some dinner in the tent, the wood stashed there nice and dry. He was uncomfortable doing it, the smells of cooking providing temptation for any bear wandering nearby to come in for a bite, but he had no choice.

He fried some Spam and ate some canned green beans along with it, then treated himself to some fruit cocktail right out of the can. Afterwards, he took the empty cans out to the cooking ring to be burned later, and called it a night.

The rain had let up completely sometime in the early morning hours. Denny woke up, needing to answer the call of nature. As he was rising from his cot, he froze. Something was out there, something nearby. His sense of such things, developed after years in the bush, was never wrong. He put his hand on the .44 magnum, just in case. The Winchester rifle was more powerful, but in the close confines of the tent, the revolver was much handier. Denny waited, listening intently, his entire being on alert. Unconsciously, he rubbed the scars on his left arm, a habit he had developed since his encounter with the starving grizzly. Whenever he was deep in thought or worried about something, he would run his hand over the reminders of that episode.

Then he heard a muffled sound, or series of sounds, that seemed to be coming closer to the closed tent flap. Some large animal was going "**Wuh, wuh, wuh**," a deep breathy noise. He knew the animal then, having heard those sounds before. Denny cocked the pistol and aimed it at the tent flap, the only thing separating him from the source of the chilling sounds. Whatever was out there was very close. Caraway could feel it standing right outside the tent, and he didn't like what he sensed. Then he got a whiff of something smelling like a big, stinky, wet dog, verifying who had come visiting. A bear was definitely out there, probably considering its next move. All Denny could do was wait.

A half shadow moved outside the tent flap, then remained still. There was a moment of silence before a loud, irritated growl sounded, then another farther away, and one more for good measure, even farther out. It was then the acrid smell of ammonia wafted into the tent.

Going to the flap and opening it, Denny saw the punctured plastic bottle, mostly empty, gently swinging on the fishing line tied to the tent frame, the remainder of the potent liquid dripping out. He chuckled to himself, put the pistol down by his cot and pulled the covers up, sure the bear wouldn't return after the welcome it received. Denny slept soundly until morning, when the warming sun woke him to a clear, cloudless day.

The next few days went smoothly without incident. The rest of the roof boards were nailed in place, and the windows and door installed. Denny finished tacking tar paper around the framing, then laid up the plywood walls, putting one-by-four strips over the seams.

The roll roofing went up the next day. After tacking down an underlayment of tar paper, Caraway laid out the long strips on the ground to let them relax so they wouldn't wrinkle after being nailed down. Grabbing one end of a strip, he went up the ladder, carrying the strip hanging down over his back.

Placing the first strip horizontally so that six inches of it overlapped the ridgeline of the roof, Denny nailed it down. He put the next layer down, slipping its edge six inches under the bottom edge of the first, sealing it with tarring from a can before running another line of nails to join the two pieces. He continued until the last layer was done, then trimmed the edge about an inch past the bottom edge of the roof boards. Doing the other side of the roof the same way, by the end of the day's work the roof was finished, looking nice and even, without a bit of tar showing anywhere. Denny took pride in doing something right, even work as simplistic as this had been.

Caraway stood looking at the completed cabin shell. A basic small structure, it looked right, and barring any malicious acts by man or beast, it would be there for many years. Denny's ego didn't require recognition, praise unnecessary, save for the pat on the back he gave himself before moving on to the next chore to be done.

Denny suddenly realized it was his birthday. "Well, happy birthday to me," he thought. "I wouldn't want to spend it any other way." At that moment, he thought of Gwen, something he occasionally did. He considered that spending a birthday with her would probably be the next best thing to having it happen out in this blessed land. A funny idea came next, funny because he'd never considered such a thing. How good would it be to enjoy it with her out here? He shook his head, gently admonishing himself for having foolish notions.

Turning his thoughts back to the work at hand, he dragged the box containing the new, small, cast iron woodstove up to the cabin door. As he knew it would, it slipped in with an inch to spare on either side. Just as Denny had done on his own cabins, after setting the stove in place, he used a piece of string and a nail as a plumb line to locate the stove piping. Cutting the stovepipe hole in the roof was a straight-forward operation, as was sealing the hole with flashing and more tarring. Placing a small conical cap over the pipe completed the job.

Taking a little breather, Denny enjoyed the view from up on the roof. He had done the same thing while building his own first cabin, though the view had been different. There, he could see a great forest around him, with dominating snow-capped black mountains in the distance, on the other side of Long Bay. Here, he saw mostly open tundra, with stretches of forest breaking up the panorama. There were some high rolling hills to the north, and way in the distance to the west some misty mountains were visible. Denny became caught up in the completely wild nature of the place he was in, the vastness of it all. He sensed that this country had been created and was functioning according to some grand scheme. It wasn't the first time Alaska had drawn out spiritual feelings from the homesteader.

The building of the little hunting shack seemed appropriate, certainly if compared to the grossly excessive masses of concrete, steel, glass, and plastic in cities. Even the dull green color of the roofing would blend in if seen from above.

Denny called it a day, planning to paint the cabin in the morning with the dark brown paint O'Bannion had provided. Afterwards, he had only to construct bunks for the clients and guides, and put up one counter for general use and his part in this would be done. The rest would come later, probably by chopper — items such as tables and chairs.

Twelve days after his arrival, including the rain delay, Denny was done, the cabin ready for the season. Insulation would be installed before the fall turned cold, unnecessary until then. In really cold times, no one would be there to need it.

Switching on the field radio, Denny called in for his flight to the next cabin site to repeat the whole process. Later that afternoon, Caraway heard the familiar sound of a light aircraft coming in. He watched the Cessna touch down on the small lake. The rolled-up tent and sheet metal stove was already stashed under the platform, and all the supplies and equipment he needed to take with him to the next site were stacked and waiting by the lakeshore. As he stood on the shore, he watched several caribou, all bulls, walking along the hills behind the lake. They were moving upward to gain higher altitude and hopefully a stiff breeze, to give them a little respite from the bugs stressing them out with their constant attacks.

Denny greeted the pilot, and loaded up the plane with his gear. Within minutes they were lifting off the water, headed east. Denny got a glimpse of the cabin he had built, thanks to the pilot circling once to give him the opportunity to admire what he'd done. It did look good. As they flew off, Denny spotted a good-sized bear walking in the direction of the cabin. He wondered if the bear had ever tasted ammonia.

It only took 30 minutes to arrive at the new site. Caraway knew it would have taken several days to get there by foot, and without the load of supplies the plane carried so easily.

This hunting camp was right off another lake shore. The process of landing on a small lake and unloading was repeated. A few minutes later he was alone again, grateful for the peace and quiet after the plane's departure. Now, the sound of the breeze, more felt than heard, and the pleasant trills of nearby birds, were all he could hear.

This stretch of country was flatter than the last, with some mountains far in the distance and barely any hills to speak of. There was a shallow draw about fifty yards from the designated cabin site. Denny didn't like that fact, because some animal, particularly a bear, could come up through the depression without being seen until it was right across from the cabin to be built. It wasn't Denny's call, however. This is where O'Bannion wanted the hunting shack, so that was all there was to it.

Once again, Denny set up the tent as he had at the last location. He saw there were two twenty-pound propane tanks, a small propane heater, and a Coleman stove. He would much rather have used wood for heat and cooking. Looking around, he saw there wasn't any nearby viable source of firewood. He placed the stove on its stand in the tent, along with one of the twenty-pound propane tanks. He was once again ready to build.

This looked to be a great place for caribou and bear hunting. As he considered this, a wolf called in the distance. Denny took the pair of small binoculars from his pack to scan the area. Even so, he couldn't spot the source of the sound. There were certainly many places of hiding for a fox, wolf, or even a bear. He wasn't looking to satisfy his curiosity. He simply wanted to know what was around, so he might be prepared for it, if necessary.

Denny checked out all the building supplies, placed under tarps as they had been at the other hunting camp. Everything seemed in order. He took the chainsaw over to the tent, and sitting on the edge of the low wooden floor platform under the open front of the tent, he cleaned, fueled, and oiled the machine, then tightened and sharpened the chain. It was an older saw, with a rough exterior, but it was a high quality brand and, much like the old snowmobile he had gotten from George Levine, the funky appearance belied its solid mechanical condition. Denny was capable of making precise cuts with it, necessary to build a good cabin.

Caraway made himself a couple of peanut butter and honey sandwiches for dinner, washing them down with hot tea. He really slathered on the peanut butter, loving the stuff, and putting enough honey on the bread so it dripped all around the edges while he ate. His grandfather had turned him on to peanut butter. His mother hadn't considered it good food, only good if you couldn't afford anything else, but Denny could sit and eat spoonful after spoonful of the gooey stuff, if he was in the mood.

He was relaxing with a pipeful of tobacco when the sound of a single-engine plane coming closer caught his attention. He went outside the tent, pipe in hand, to see the Cessna 180 he had flown in on come down and land on the lake. Taxiing up to where he stood, he was surprised to see Carlton O'Bannion step out. The pilot kept the engine running.

Shaking hands with Denny, O'Bannion told him he had seen the first cabin and was satisfied, and he needed him to get this one done as soon as possible.

"When do you want it to be finished?" Denny asked.

"I need it done and ready in nine days. Can you do it, or should I bring in someone else to help?"

"No, I can do it. What's up?"

With an impatient look on his face, O'Bannion said, "I have a last-minute client coming who paid me a bonus to put him on a bear hunt right away. Is that okay with you?"

Though Denny didn't like O'Bannon's tone, the man was obviously under some pressure, so he let it go.

"I'll have it ready in time."

Turning and walking away, O'Bannion said, "All right then, Caraway, see to it."

The unpleasant guide got back into the plane. Denny watched it taxi away and take off. He'd start early the next morning and get the shack done on time. He was rankled by Carlton's attitude, and would be glad when the job was over.

Chapter Fifteen

It was overcast the next morning, with a steady ten-mile-an- hour wind blowing. Putting his raingear on after a quick breakfast, Denny set to work. Luckily, except for some drizzle, no heavy rain came, so the work went smoothly. In a day and a half, the platform was finished and two days more had the wall framing up and the roof started. Denny spent long hours to get the hunting shack done in the nine days. He was more interested in getting it finished to be able to leave O'Bannion's employ, rather than doing so to complete a worthwhile project. This was one situation he had no desire to remain in any longer than was necessary.

He was halfway finished with the roof boards when the rain came back, but he had to keep going to meet the demanded deadline. Caraway hadn't been in such a situation since he'd been a rep for the advertising company he had worked for in Reno, when he was under constant pressure to have things "all wrapped up" on time. He knew working for someone else again would not be enjoyable, and now longed to be back on the homestead, alone, and content to be so.

Denny cut several boards to length standing under the finished roof covering, then took them up. He was almost finished when, climbing down the wet ladder, he slipped and fell backwards, landing flat on his back, knocking the wind out of him. Luckily his foot hadn't caught between rungs or it could have been worse. He lay there a minute, waiting for something to hurt. Nothing did.

Rising up, he seemed fine. However, Denny saw he had missed hitting his head on a rock by mere inches. Walking around to see if anything of his was damaged, and finding he was fit, Denny picked up another board and tried to continue working, but it was raining buckets, and he had to stop until the downpour let up.

Now, he appreciated the propane heater, which was easy to start and quickly warmed up the tent, with the front flap part way open for ventilation. He'd called it a day around ten p.m., eaten some hot dogs and beans before turning in, falling asleep almost immediately. Any curious bears were on their own.

Caraway awoke to a clear sky with the sun shining brightly. Not wanting to waste a minute, foregoing breakfast, Denny got to work. It was day six. By the end of the day the roof was finished, and the two windows and door installed. He took an hour break, then started on the outer wall sheathing. The plywood went quickly and was well on the way to being done. Denny was beat, and was half asleep while eating his dinner, dropping onto the cot right after putting the cooking pot and plate out by the cook fly.

When Denny woke up the next morning, the little metal cook pot was not where he had left it. Neither could he locate the food canister. After searching for a while he located the stainless steel pot on the other side of the new cabin site. It was all dented up, but had no actual holes in it, and was licked perfectly clean.

The food canister took a little longer to find, and it was by pure luck he noticed it in the lake, floating about five feet from shore. It was scratched up, but had no other damage to it, and was still closed. Denny laughed to himself about the little canister and how he knew a bear or other predator could leave it somewhere far away on the tundra.

Back at the work site, he found the installed roof boards were dry enough to cover, so the tarpaper and rolled roofing went on. Denny pressed on to start painting the place the same deep brown as the first shack. The next day he finished the painting, and built the bunk beds and counter. It was almost one in the morning when he was finished, exhausted. He was glad the weather had held until he was done. He gulped down some cold beans and bread with a cup of instant coffee, after which he repeated the familiar process of lying down on the cot and dropping off to sleep in minutes.

Chapter Sixteen

Caraway stood admiring his work, complete and ready to use as he had promised, on the ninth day. He moved the propane heater and Coleman stove into the shack, took down the tent as before, and waited for O'Bannion to arrive. It was barely half an hour later when the Cessna came in. Denny walked over to the lake to greet his boss, the client, and the assistant guide. Caraway was all packed up and ready to head for home.

When the plane's door opened, only O'Bannion and one other man stepped out, and he was definitely not the assistant guide. He was about five foot six and weighed, by Denny's estimation, at least two hundred and fifty pounds. He was wearing new outdoor clothing, looking like African safari garb, the jacket a tight fit. To top it all off, he wore an Australian-looking hat with one side pinned up. He had on rolled-down hip waders he was probably wearing when the plane took off. All Denny could do was mentally shake his head.

Caraway had a feeling O'Bannion was going to have an interesting hunt. He went to help the pilot unload, when O'Bannion took him aside, a tense look on his face. "Caraway, I have a problem and need you to stay on for this hunt. My assistant guide walked out on me and you have to fill in for him. I'll pay you what I would have paid Jerry plus a bonus if you do, but you have to stay and guide Mr. Goulsby on this hunt."

Caraway took the tone in O'Bannion's words and the look in his eye as almost a threat, which he didn't appreciate one bit. He didn't react as he normally would though, facing off with the man and getting things straight. He wanted to, but he could certainly use the extra money and knew he could do the job. Swallowing his anger, he told O'Bannion, "I'll do it, but you'll have to find someone else for the next hunt. This one I'll do, and no more. After this, I'm quits."

"Yeah, fine, fine," O'Bannion said. "Just help the pilot finish unloading and get the client settled in. I've got to get back and find another guide. Can you handle it?"

Denny hadn't expected to be left alone like this with a client he knew nothing about, and regretted having agreed to the hunt. Denny knew he could work this country for a good bear, which is what the client had come for. He nodded his response to O'Bannion's last question. Turning away, Denny's boss went over to the client while Denny unloaded the man's gear from the plane, his jaw muscles working overtime.

Caraway thought for a minute about doing another hunt if O'Bannion still hadn't found a new assistant guide by the time this one was over. He expected to be well paid for helping out, but already had a strong sense that getting his full payment from O'Bannion might be difficult. He had the man sized up by now. He decided to see how this bear hunt turned out before making a final decision.

As they got all the gear from the plane, the pilot asked Denny if he had ever worked for O'Bannion before and when Denny answered no, the pilot told him to be sure he got his pay on time, if he could. "The man has a reputation, but you didn't hear it from me."

A few minutes later the plane was gone, leaving Caraway and the client alone, the hunter giving Denny a quizzical look. Denny carried the man's duffle over to the cabin and gave him his choice of which bunk he wanted to sleep on. He chose the lower one, and Denny took the other lower bunk on the other side of the one-room shack.

"So, when is Mr. O'Bannion returning," asked the client. "I want to get out there early tomorrow."

Denny noted the man's thick eastern accent, probably New York or New Jersey. "Actually, I'll be taking you out on the hunt tomorrow myself. Mr. O'Bannion had some pressing business to attend to."

"Probably has to replace the lazy sumbitch who walked out at the airport. Have you ever guided before?"

Denny thought a minute before answering. "I've been hunting in Alaska for over ten years."

"You didn't answer my question; have you ever guided someone else?"

"In all honesty, I haven't. You needn't worry, Mr. Goulsby, we'll get you a good bear."

"I didn't spend no fifteen grand to have an assistant take me out, I want O'Bannion himself to do it!"

The guy was getting red in the face, obviously pissed about the situation, though no more than Denny himself. Avoiding unpleasant situations such as this, as he'd had to deal with many times in the past, was one of the main reasons he was living the solitary life of a homesteader, but he held his temper and told the man he could call O'Bannion and reschedule for another hunt, probably next year, or go out with him and get a bear.

Mr. Goulsby, not wanting to lose his opportunity for a hunt, agreed to give Denny a chance. Glaring at Caraway, he said, "If I don't get a good grizzly, you'll find out who you're dealing with."

Denny was not impressed. He simply nodded and went about preparing dinner, pan frying a couple of steaks, cooking some canned green beans and buttering thick slices of bread.

Goulsby sat silently on his bunk giving Denny the evil eye, not saying anything. If he thought this would bother him, he was wrong. Caraway was relieved the man had opted not to talk. The silence lasted through dinner, of which Caraway had little, the rotund client eating the lion's share of the meat and beans and five slices of heavily buttered bread. By dinner's end, his safari jacket wasn't spotless anymore.

After the meal, Goulsby went outside to smoke a cigarette, and Denny went down to the lake to wash dishes. As he was finishing up, returning to the cabin, Goulsby came quickly waddling up to him, a set of large, expensive binoculars hung around his neck that were bumping his belly as he trotted over to Denny. Loudly whispering, he said, "I saw a bear, I saw a bear!"

Caraway had him point out where he saw the bruin. Scanning the area through the client's binoculars, he saw a small female grizzly with two cubs about two hundred and fifty yards away.

"Is that the bear you saw, Mr. Goulsby?"

Looking through the binoculars, Goulsby excitedly said, "Yeah, it is, shall we go after it?"

Denny explained to him it was a small female bear with cubs and they weren't going after them.

Goulsby looked through the glasses again, and apparently saw the cubs this time. "Well, it still looks like a good bear to me."

There were some bugs out, and Goulsby trotted back to the cabin waving his arms around his head. Denny had half a mind to stay in the tent for the night, then figured he might as well see it through and not make things worse than they already were. Besides, he knew he would sleep better in the shack, and he needed to be alert the next day. He stayed outside a while, long enough to smoke a pipe, which helped him relax and avoid the irritating client. Glassing while outside, he saw on a far rise what appeared to be a big bear, maybe half a mile away. He'd check out the area in the morning with his client. With luck the big bruiser might still be around.

Fortunately, when Denny entered the shack, the cantankerous Goulsby was already sleeping, snoring like a freight train. It took Denny a while to fall asleep, a couple of wads of tissue paper stuck in his ears helping him to finally get some rest.

Chapter Seventeen

Denny was up at five thirty, made a pot of coffee on the Coleman, and began cooking some eggs and bacon, being sure to make a big batch. Once the bacon was cooking, Goulsby woke up, stretched, farted loudly, and went outside to relieve himself.

He seemed in a better mood, and talked with Denny about his experiences living in Alaska. The client had never been in the north country before. He had apparently shot deer in the eastern woods, and that was the extent of his hunting.

Trying to make some light conversation, Caraway asked him what he did for a living.

Goulsby gave him a hard look and said, "I'm in import-export."

Denny let it drop.

By seven, they were out hiking towards the area where Denny had seen the bear the night before. Though it was only half a mile away, halfway there Goulsby insisted they take a break. When he started lighting a cigarette, Denny told him an animal could detect a cigarette from a long distance, and the smell might run it out of the area. The client gave him a sour look and flipped the smoke into some willows. Denny went over and extinguished the cigarette.

"These bugs are driving me nuts," Goulsby said. The sound of him slapping his clothes and trying to kill some of the mosquitoes was pretty loud and Denny finally had to tell him to stop.

"Put some of this bug dope on; it will help a lot." Denny offered him his bottle.

"That stuff might give me a rash."

"Well, Mr. Goulsby, if you keep slapping at the bugs, you'll probably spook anything shootable. So, which is it to be, a rash or a bear?"

Taking the bottle from Denny, the sweating man spread some on his face necks and hands.

Soon after they continued walking, Goulsby complained, "These hip boots are killing me. Can you go back and get me the hiking shoes from my pack?"

Denny couldn't help giving the man a look, which wasn't lost on Goulsby, who told him to forget it. "Let's just get my bear."

Denny had been glassing the area for a while from the rise where he had seen the bear walking, when he spotted a large grizzly moving in the willows about three hundred yards away, possibly the one he had seen the night before. It looked to be an old bear, with the slow rolling gait a mature, confident male would have. He told the client there was a big bear nearby and they would work around the rise they were on and try to come up on it from the left. Goulsby got all excited and began to move away. Denny gripped his arm and told him to stay right behind him and be as quiet as possible. The man nodded quickly.

It took about half an hour for Denny to position them so Goulsby could make a clear shot, about seventy-five yards from the big interior grizzly. It should have been simple, easy, but when Goulsby aimed his fancy heavy magnum rifle, he shot too fast and hit the bear too far back. Roaring and snapping at the spot the bullet had entered, the bear took off through the willows, and was quickly out of sight. When Denny had yelled to Goulsby to hit him again, the man simply stood there saying, "I hit him, I hit him!" Denny had gotten one shot off with his 30-06, and was sure he had connected, but the animal hadn't even reacted to the shot.

What should have been a quick successful hunt had turned into the worst case for a guide. A wounded big bear and a client he couldn't rely on to hold his sand.

Scanning the direction the bear had gone in, Caraway was lucky enough to see it break out of a willow patch and then drop down out of sight. He got a gut feeling the grizz was going to stay put and wait for its attackers to come to him, then get some payback for the pain they had caused.

"Let's go after him, Caraway!" Goulsby yelled in Denny's ear.

It was all Denny could do to keep from grabbing him by the collar and shaking him. Instead, getting right in Goulsby's face, staring directly into his eyes, he told the man, "You're going to shut up and do exactly as I say or you'll be going back to the cabin and wait until I'm done cleaning up this mess, do you understand?"

The Caraway look stopped the man from his raving, and he calmed down enough to listen to what Denny told him.

He explained they were going to wait for an hour, to let the hurt bear stiffen up or, if they were lucky, to die from its wounds. Then they were slowly and carefully going to track the animal to where it was lying and do what was necessary. "You stay ten feet behind me and follow until I tell you to do something else."

Goulsby nodded.

Caraway found a good place to scope out the area where the bear was last seen and kept watch in case the bear went on the move. Goulsby sat behind him, smoking and acting agitated. Caraway was worried, partly about keeping this guy safe, and partly about not getting shot in the back by the damn fool in the heat of the moment.

An hour passed and they headed out, Denny in the lead. He took his time and circled around far enough out to hopefully keep from arousing the bear. Finally, they were behind the place he had last seen it. He told Goulsby to circle around about twenty-five yards away and wait. "If the bear comes out, and he will come in a hurry, shoot him. Don't wait for me to shoot, but shoot the bear, not me."

Goulsby nodded, a wide-eyed look on his face. Denny knew the man didn't want to be anywhere near the bear when it came.

Denny hadn't gone thirty yards towards where the bear was apparently waiting, wounded, when the animal reacted. Letting out a huge roar, it came for Denny. Caraway was ready, and prayed Goulsby would react properly. As soon as the bear cleared the bushes, Denny fired a shot just beneath its chin. The bear dropped, then got right back up again. "Shoot!" Denny yelled, just before putting another one-hundred-and-eighty grain bullet into the bear's chest as it rose. He didn't hear a shot from Goulsby's direction. The bear turned around after being hit again and disappeared back into the brush, still roaring loudly.

Standing there for a moment, rifle raised and ready, Denny chanced a look in his client's direction. Goulsby was standing there, his rifle held in both hands in front of him. He seemed frozen in place. Watching the bushes, Denny walked sideways over to where Goulsby still stood unmoving, a totally blank look on his face. Denny shook him by the arm and the fear-filled hunter jerked at the touch, then looked at Denny and said, "Did you get him?"

Disgusted, Denny took the man's big magnum from him and handed him his trusty old '06. Loosening the quick detachable mounts and removing the scope, Denny asked Goulsby how the iron sights were adjusted.

He answered, "Twenty-five yards."

Removing his pack and leaving it and the scope on the ground by Goulsby's feet and getting right in the man's face again, he said, "Goulsby, don't do a damn thing. Just stand right here. If the bear comes at you, try and take a shot with the Winchester."

Goulsby simply nodded.

Turning, Denny went towards the willows once again, cursing under his breath, the big rifle feeling unfamiliar in his hands. He hoped things would go right. Speaking in a whisper, Caraway said, "Gramps, if you're there, I could use a hand on this one."

Coming to within ten yards of the willows, Denny picked up a rock and tossed it in the direction the bear had taken. No response. He could see a tunnel going through the bushes, a bear trail worked into the willows over years of use. There was nothing left to do but follow.

Denny had the metallic taste of fear in his mouth. Still, he pressed on. Stopping suddenly, Caraway thought he saw a large, dark shape in front of him off the right side of the trail. It wasn't moving. Denny took two more steps, rifle at the ready, and he could see the bear's form, head up, facing him. The animal was still alive, but too sick to move. It lowered its head, and quickly sighting the rifle, Denny fired a round to strike the bear's neck squarely, just below the head. A spasm went through the animal, and a long release of air came from its lungs, almost a moan. It was over.

Working another round into the gun's chamber, Denny waited for several minutes before approaching the animal and poking the muzzle at its open eye. It was dead.

Denny came out of the willows to find Goulsby standing exactly as he had been when he left him to finish the bear. He was disgusted. "Come help me," was all he said. Goulsby followed obediently to where the bear was lying.

It was a long and difficult process, skinning out the bear where it lay in the brush, getting no help from the client. Denny was glad, not wanting to have anything to do with Goulsby, and he worked steadily until the job was done. Loading the heavy hide on his pack rack, Denny and the now subdued client headed back to the cabin. No words were passed between the two men as they silently hiked along. Once back at camp, Goulsby went inside while Denny spread out the hide hair side down and thoroughly coated the skin side with salt. Rolling it up into a neat bundle, he stashed in under the cabin in the shade, inside a large game bag. Denny called the pilot to let him know the hunt was over and to please come get the client. The pilot said they'd come in early the next morning.

The evening went well enough, at least for Denny. Scant conversation and a quiet meal. Trying to make the best of it, Denny told Goulsby he had a good trophy to take home with him.

Goulsby gave him a sharp look, lit up another cigarette, then stood looking out the window, his back to Denny. Caraway went outside to square away his things still in the tent, resolved this was going to be his last hunt for or with anyone else.

Early the next morning the plane came. Goulsby had been packed up and waiting for several hours. Caraway figured the man wanted to get away from him as soon as possible, his ego deflated. He offered to help with the client's bags, and was refused with a simple "No thanks." Shrugging his shoulders, Denny wished him a good trip home and went into the tent to gather his own gear.

O'Bannion came in a few minutes later, obviously upset, his face beet red.

"What happened here, Caraway! Goulsby said he'd never hunt with me again. Told me he had a rough time with you, and suggested I get an assistant with more consideration for a customer."

"I'm not surprised. Well, he can relax, I'm done guiding, for you or anyone else."

"What are you talking about? I need you to stay on longer. I couldn't get anyone to fill in for Jerry yet."

"Mr. O'Bannion, I told you I would do this one hunt to help you out. Now I'm through. I was obligated to build you the two cabins and did you a favor staying with an inexperienced hunter, a spineless man, who could well have gotten me killed yesterday. I wouldn't hunt rabbits with the guy. I'm just glad one of us isn't hurt or dead."

"Dammit, sometimes that's the way a hunt goes. Just part of the business. Can't you handle it?"

"O'Bannion, if I couldn't handle it, a grizzly bear skin wouldn't be stashed under the cabin. I'm just not interested. I'm going to need a flight back to Fairbanks once the client is deposited at the airport, if you wouldn't mind. I'd appreciate you sending my pay to the P.O. box I gave you."

"If you don't have the decency to help me out and do another hunt, you'll get your check at season's end and not before."

Denny stepped forward, until he was a few inches from O'Bannion's face, and said, "I really wouldn't do that, if I were you."

Carlton stood his ground for a few seconds, but the obvious anger and resolve in Caraway's intense stare had the effect it usually did. O'Bannion turned and walked out of the tent, then turned and yelled, "If you don't stay on, you can find your own way home." He was sure Denny would give in to his ultimatum. But he didn't know the man.

"Suits me, O'Bannion, but I better have my money soon, or I'll find you and we'll get squared away."

The guide, shaking with anger, cursed at Denny and stomped back to the airplane. Denny didn't know what he told the pilot, and a few minutes later the plane was headed out, and Denny was alone in the camp.

Fixing himself a cup of tea, and lighting up another bowl of pipe tobacco, Denny gave himself time to calm down and consider the situation. He had the feeling O'Bannion wasn't kidding. He decided to wait until the end of the next day to be sure the plane wasn't back for him. It was actually pleasant being alone in the camp despite the situation. Denny settled in for the evening. Some food, a mug of tea, and another pipeful of good tobacco had a calming effect on him, and he soon drifted off to sleep.

Caraway woke the next morning to a welcome silence. No snoring, no complaining. Going down to the little lake, he had a bracing wash up in the cold water that had him wide awake by the time he was done. He had a big breakfast that would have done Goulsby justice, then stayed in with the screened windows open, reading a book he had brought, waiting for the sound of the Cessna coming in.

By late afternoon, Denny decided O'Bannion had indeed left him to his own devices. He could have called him on the phone, then thought better of it, not wanting to give the man an opportunity to try and force him into another hunt. No, he'd make his own way out of the area. He wasn't particularly worried about getting to the Richardson Highway to the east, he was simply pissed off at O'Bannion for deserting him. The guide had shown his true colors, and they weren't pretty. Denny would settle with him when he got back to Fairbanks. He had no doubt he'd get there. It might even be a good trek.

Chapter Eighteen

Early the next morning, Denny set out. He had all the gear he needed to make the trip, and had enough food for three days' travel, which he figured would be enough to make it to the highway. Stepping out of the cabin, he took a sighting from his old compass, locating a few degrees north of dead east. Adjusting the pistol on his hip and the pack on his back, taking his rifle in hand, the homesteader started out.

The first day went much as he had expected, hiking over wide areas of tundra, crossing numerous small streams, and working his way cautiously through willow thickets. Caraway moved carefully to avoid possible injury. He planned on having a smooth, steady walk out, though he knew that in the bush anything could happen.

Surprisingly, he saw no large game the first day, only some birds and a couple of hares. He did come across several piles of bear scat, not fresh and no worry.

Mid-day, he stopped briefly to have something to eat to keep his strength up. He started a small fire, adding green wood to make smoke and keep the bugs at bay, so he could enjoy his sandwich in peace. He sat, not really thinking about anything, merely chewing and resting. Finished, he took out a piece of moose jerky to chew while walking, hoisted his pack, and after taking another compass sighting, continued on.

When Denny was tired enough to stop, he found a spot by the edge of a creek where he could use the plastic tarp he brought to make a shelter, draping it over an opening in some willows.

Gathering what wood he'd need to cook a little meal and keep the chill off, he settled in for the evening, even though it was full daylight, being the longest day of summer. The light didn't stop Caraway from dozing off. It had been a long walk from the hunting camp, and the wide expanses of muskeg he had to cross were no joy to walk on. You never knew how deep your foot would sink, the solidity of each step varying.

Smoking his pipe, Denny felt fine, doing the thing he loved best, wandering in beautiful Alaskan country. Though he had been forced into taking this hike, that fact was secondary to the pleasure he felt being in the best place he knew. His pipe out, Denny dozed off.

Several hours later he woke up, his sixth sense alerting him to something being around. He put his hand on the butt of his .44 and listened carefully. He heard a quick scurrying sound close behind him, and waited. A moment later, a red fox peeped its head around the willows in front of Denny, just a few feet away. The animal stood unmoving, only his head in view, watching Denny where he sat. Denny quietly said, "Hello Mr. fox, any luck hunting this evening?"

The fox didn't even flinch at the sound of a human voice. It kept watching him, a sly, intelligent look on its face. Denny sat watching the animal until it finally withdrew beyond his view, though Denny had the feeling it wasn't far away. Hoping the fox would be the only animal to disturb his sleep, he nodded off again.

Denny awoke a brief while later, to the sound of something being dragged on the ground. He saw the bottom of his pack as it disappeared into the bushes. Throwing himself forward, he managed to grab one strap and retrieve it. A moment later, the fox's head appeared out of the willows, the obvious culprit in the foiled pack heist.

Smiling, Denny told the fox he needed his supplies more than it did.

The fox, sorry it hadn't made off with the prize, slunk away, a disappointed look on its face.

Stirring the coals in his fire, Denny boiled some water in his little tin can with the wire handle, made some tea, ate several more pieces of jerky, and a slice of bread with some peanut butter spread on it with two fingers.

Rising up, he worked out the kinks as best he could. It would take some walking to get rid of the stiffness in his muscles, reminding him he wasn't a young man anymore. Walking up a slight rise to get a better view of the land ahead, Denny saw forested country a mile away to the east. He looked forward to a change from the miles of tundra he had already traversed.

He hadn't been hiking long when he saw the fox trotting about fifty feet behind him. When Denny stopped to look at him, the fox stopped too. Seeing no harm in it, Denny continued on. Glancing back occasionally, he noted the fox continuing to follow along. Caraway wasn't sure why the fox was still traveling with him, especially since he hadn't given it any food. Denny had seen animals do some unusual things in the past — unexpected behavior, so he merely shrugged and continued on.

He came to a wide, fast-running creek and, having done it numerous times before, took off his boots and socks once again, rolled up his pants, and forded the icy water. On the other side, drying his feet with his bandana, he put his socks and boots back on, rolled down his pants, and pushing through a fringe of willows entered the trees ahead of him, the ones he had seen earlier. Though he thought it would make a nice change from the tundra, this was a section of forest full of blow downs and dense undergrowth. It turned out to be difficult to consistently move in the direction he wanted to go. The forest kept moving him around with obstacles. Changing direction out of necessity, he had to keep referring to the compass to stay on course.

The bugs in the trees were thicker than on the tundra where a good breeze could put them off. After putting on his head net, Denny had to be careful not to tear the fragile barrier on one of the many small broken branches sticking out from tree trunks all around him. The steady buzz of the insects added to the unpleasant atmosphere of the forest.

He had been hiking for several hours when he noticed the fox out of the corner of his eye, gliding through the trees to his left. He was surprised to see him because, when he had forded the last stream, the fox seemed put off by the water, trotting back and forth on the far bank. Denny thought he had seen the last of him, but was obviously mistaken. It was a young fox, and probably hadn't established a territory of his own yet. So here they were, two guys out for a stroll, neither of them in country they could call their own. Caraway didn't mind the little creature's company.

All day Denny kept moving, finally leaving the oppressive forested area behind, back on open ground, fording several more small creeks, avoiding boggy places, and crossing lots of tundra. Every little while he caught a glimpse of the fox tagging along, and once saw it catch a small rodent and stop to hunker down and eat its prey. Caraway kept moving, not expecting the fox to catch up to him. But soon enough, it appeared about ten yards off to his left again, seemingly pacing him as he walked.

Much as Denny enjoyed the country, by the time afternoon came around, it was becoming tedious. Walking on muskeg was wearing on him. He tried not to think about O'Bannion, the reason for this forced trek, but couldn't help wondering how it would be when he got back to Fairbanks and went to get his pay from the man. Denny intended to do whatever was necessary to get paid. He hoped O'Bannion would see the sense of paying him off right away to end the episode. Caraway would only know what was to be when he got there.

While considering a stop for the day, by mere luck he spotted a willow ptarmigan barely twenty feet away. It was a plump little hen, so Denny slowly sat down, pulled his .44 pistol out and, resting his arms on his knees, squeezed off a shot. It was perfect, the heavy bullet striking at the base of the hapless bird's neck, cleanly removing the neck and head. Now he had a real dinner. Smiling to himself at what a perfect shot it had been, he cleaned the bird, plucking the feathers as he walked. The fox, spooked by the report of the gun, ran fifty yards away to stand and see what was coming next. As Denny walked away, feathers scattering in the breeze as he went, the fox ran to the tiny gut pile and slurped it up. When the bird was clean, the homesteader dropped it into his pack and continued on.

He hadn't gone another mile when he heard an awful ruckus up ahead beyond a small mound in front of him. Walking directly to the little hillock, he kept it between him and whatever was roaring and growling behind it. He had a pretty good idea what was going on.

Sure enough, when he got to a good vantage point, having crawled as slowly as he could to see over the rise, there was a female grizzly with two cubs standing at a distance behind her, and a much larger bear facing her. They were both on their hind legs in a typical bear fighting position, with their necks outstretched and their heads jutting forward.

The big bear had probably been following the trio, hoping for an easy meal. The mama bear was having none of it. There was nothing Denny knew of as fierce and determined as a mother bear defending her young, and her attitude was not lost on the male bear who seemed to be having some second thoughts. Just as he turned his head away a few degrees, the female lunged at him, quick as only a bear can be, actually knocking the big male backwards onto the ground. Though the boar got up quickly, it was clear he was through. His head turned, and keeping an eye on the female, he cautiously sidled away.

The sow didn't move towards him, but kept watch until the male had walked away up a long slope to Denny's left, which was fine with Caraway.

He was glad the bear, in an obviously bad mood, hadn't headed in his direction. Denny slipped away out of sight of the female and walked to the southeast, checking his old compass to stay on track.

Heavy dark clouds had been building, and Denny knew he was going to get wet. He made for a large outcropping of lichen-covered rocks up ahead, hoping to find a little shelter.

Luckily, there was enough of an overhang on one side to at least keep him out of the worst of the rain to come. Denny gathered what small wood he could find that would burn, got a fire going, and soon had the bird from his pack skewered on a willow stalk over the flames. It was almost fully cooked when big drops began to fall, and within a few minutes the small fire was totally out. Denny tucked his tarp around him to wait it out, gnawing on the mostly cooked meat as the skies opened up. The rain was heavy and strong, and despite his slight shelter and the tarp, Denny was soon miserably wet, though no longer hungry, having polished off every little bit of the tough bird.

Walking all day had taken its toll. Caraway drifted in and out of a light, fitful sleep as the rain continued. He didn't look forward to repeating the process of slogging over the tundra the next day. O'Bannion was at the top of his black list.

The rain finally let up, though there was heavy overcast. Denny could have used a couple of hours more sleep, but instead got his stuff together and headed out. Figuring he might reach the road in another day, perhaps two, Caraway had no concerns, though in the back of his mind there still remained an edge of anger, brought on by O'Bannion's hard, unreasonable attitude.

Chapter Nineteen

Denny knew he couldn't be more than ten or twelve miles from the highway. Except for watching the two bears facing off and the fox keeping him company, it had simply been a steady slogging through typical bush country. Soon, according to his calculations and with the use of his grandfather's compass, he'd be well out of it. He had a sudden, powerful desire for a big juicy burger from the North Star Cafe, and promised himself to get one once he got back, along with several cups of freshly brewed coffee.

An unnatural sound entered his hearing. It took him a moment to figure out what it was. It was getting louder as he stood listening, the sound of a light aircraft in distress, the stuttering of an engine not running right. The sound of the failing engine suddenly stopped completely. Then he saw it: a small airplane coming down at a steep angle. All he could do was watch, the total lack of sound adding an eeriness to the scene. The plane disappeared before it crashed.

Denny estimated it was about a mile away, perhaps a little farther. He set out at a steady trot in its direction, as steady a jog as the muskeg allowed. The fox was startled by his change of pace, and moved away before following again at a distance.

It took Denny about fifteen minutes to get to the crash site, and he saw why the plane had disappeared when it had come down. It had dropped into a shallow draw with a creek running through it. It looked as if the plane had caught a wing tip and cart wheeled once or twice. Both wings were broken off and lying a short distance away, one across the other. The crumpled tail section was almost torn off the plane, hanging to one side, while the propeller was twisted and useless. One wheel was thirty yards down the creek, having bounced and rolled after impact.

The fuselage was lying in the creek on its side, facing upstream, the pilot's seat on the downside. Water was running into the plane through the broken windshield and door.

Denny slid down the embankment and ran to the plane. He saw the pilot still in his seat and knew it was probably too late for him. His head and shoulder were under water. Gently lifting his head, he felt for a neck pulse. The man was gone.

The female passenger sitting next to him was above the surface, held in place by the seat belt. Walking around to the other side, he climbed up, pried open the door and carefully cut the belt with his knife. Holding onto the unconscious woman's arm, the severed belt allowed him to extract her from the plane. Just as he got her laid out on the bank of the stream, she regained consciousness and screamed out in pain. Denny patted her on the shoulder, and slipped his pack under her head. Denny spoke quietly to her, telling the woman she was safe now and should try to relax. The woman, in her mid-thirties, kept moaning about her leg. Denny saw it was clearly broken, though he didn't see any protruding bones. She had some blood on her forehead, but, when Denny wiped it away, there was only a slight cut. Along with a bruise on her cheek, that was all that was visible. She had been lucky, more so than the unfortunate pilot.

By now, the bugs had homed in on them. Denny took his head net and an aluminized emergency blanket from the pack, careful not to disturb her too much when he took it out from under her head. After putting the head net on the woman and covering her with the blanket, he put some bug dope on himself.

Going back to the plane, Denny got the pilot out and laid him nearby, behind a patch of willows, so the woman wouldn't see him. Then he returned once again to the plane. After switching on the radio he was relieved to find it still functioning. There was a small label with the emergency frequency printed on it. Denny switched to it and called for help. He got a quick response and told them what had happened, describing their location as best he could. Returning to the woman, still conscious and in obvious pain, Denny built a fire nearby, adding green branches once it got going, to make a visible signal. He gave the woman, whose name was Caroline Barker, some clean water from his water bottle.

Not much for small talk, he tried to keep her mind off the pain in her leg. His efforts didn't go unnoticed.

She put a hand on his arm and gave him a grateful look. "It was amazing and wonderful you were nearby when we crashed. I don't believe in coincidence. I know you probably saved my life." Caroline smiled at him.

Denny could see she was a strong person, dealing with the situation as well as could be expected. They talked about their lives, and she was fascinated with Caraway's description of his way of living and how he had come to be on his homestead, though he omitted a number of things she needn't know about.

Caroline was a teacher being flown out to McGrath to start a job there. She had been a teacher in the villages for ten years, mostly substituting for other teachers. This job was to be fulltime and long term. Now, it appeared it was not to be.

Denny told her it seemed as if life sometimes "had other plans for us we don't know about until they happen."

A sudden increase in pain caused her to moan and grip his arm tightly until it subsided. Denny felt a pang in his gut. Except for his last visit with Gwenny some time ago, he hadn't had any real contact with a woman, and never in a situation such as this. Caroline was attractive, with good looks Denny thought of as "natural," no make-up or fancy hair style, with a healthy, clean, clear-eyed appearance. She also had a pair of beautiful green eyes that went well with her blonde hair. Denny had to break away from his observations to pay attention to the present situation.

"Oh, look," Caroline said, "there's a fox up on the bank." Sure enough, there was Denny's fox staring down on them, not willing to come closer, the plane wreck and the two other figures putting him off, Denny's presence holding him there all the same. Denny told her about the fox and how he had come to be out on the tundra, with his "furry sidekick," as he put it.

He was surprised to see Caroline get an angry look on her face when he told her about being left to find his way out, though he didn't mention O'Bannion by name. Despite the present situation, what was obviously a wrong act in her mind angered her. Denny was impressed with Caroline, there was no doubt. She saw him observing her and they paused in time, looking at each other the way people sometimes do when the connection has become stronger through the circumstance they are in. Denny actually smiled a real smile, which she returned openly.

At that moment, the sound of a helicopter coming in broke them out of their intimate moment. Denny threw some more green branches on the fire, but they had already been spotted.

A few minutes later, they were safely stashed on the chopper, the pilot's body covered and strapped onto a basket on one side of the fuselage. As they turned to head back to Fairbanks, Denny caught a glimpse of the fox trotting out onto the tundra, continuing the daily struggle of survival, the connection between them now in the past and of no further interest to the little predator.

After days spent hiking, the quick flight to Fairbanks was anticlimactic, though Denny wasn't complaining. They landed on the helipad at Fairbanks memorial, and Caroline was whisked away to be cared for. At first, the nurses thought Denny was involved in the crash, until he explained how he had come to be in the vicinity. They were a little doubtful at first, then amazed and not a little impressed, though such stories aren't unheard of in Alaska. Unusual and potentially life-threatening situations were par for the course in the north country. Truth to tell, Denny'd had more than the usual share of adventures during his ten years in Alaska. He had come to take his wild existence in stride, though this plane crash had been something unique, even for him.

He asked one of the nurses if there was some place in the hospital he could clean up. At close quarters, his unbathed condition, after days on the tundra, had not gone unnoticed. One of the nurses took him to the doctors locker room, gave him a towel, soap, and shampoo and left him to wash away all the footsore miles. After getting dressed in the one set of clean clothes in his pack, Denny went down to the hospital cafeteria and wolfed down a tray full of food.

Before he left the hospital to get back to his truck, Denny dropped by Caroline's room to say good-bye. When he knocked on the closed door, a tall, rugged-looking man in his early fifties opened the door and said, "You must be Mr. Caraway, I'm Nathan Barker, Caroline's father. Please come in."

Caroline was awake and seemed to be settled comfortably in the hospital bed. She had been freshened up after having her leg set and cast and, considering the situation, looked good to Denny's eyes. She smiled when she saw him and extended her hand. He walked over and took it without hesitation. They remained like that for a moment, Caroline smiling and Denny admiring the view, until Mr. Barker cleared his throat. Denny turned to him and Barker thanked Caraway, saying how grateful he was to him for helping his daughter, probably saving her from greater harm. Denny simply nodded.

Then Caroline said, "Daddy, remember what we discussed?"

"Oh, yes, Caroline said you might be in need of employment. Your last job, I take it, didn't end well?"

"You could say so, Mr. Barker. I haven't settled with the man I was working for yet, and I hope it won't be any more difficult than necessary."

The look in Caraway's eyes backed up his words. Instead of putting him off, it impressed Barker. He had lived in Alaska a long time, met a lot of people he could do without, and a few he was glad to know. He had a feeling, despite having just met Caraway, that he would fall into the latter category.

"Well, may I call you Denny?"

Caraway nodded.

"Denny, I own a large surveying company based in Fairbanks and Anchorage. I contract work all over Alaska, quite a bit for the state. I can always use a reliable man on my crew in the remote areas where we work. With your experience living in the wilderness, I think you could do a good job as bear guard and, well, overseeing my crew in general while in the bush. You'd be well paid and your needs would be met, whatever you require for the job. Interested? I could start you in a few days."

Denny liked Barker's direct way of putting things, and figured he'd treat him fairly. And besides, he was Caroline's father. Caraway was also aware the job Barker offered might not have existed before his daughter had explained Denny's situation.

Caroline spoke up again, something she obviously had no problem doing. "My daddy's a fair man, Denny. You should consider it."

Again, Denny gave Caroline one of his rare full smiles and told her he had already decided. He'd take the job. His homestead was all locked down anyway, and he could pick up whatever he needed in Fairbanks.

"May I ask who you were last working for, Denny, prior to the plane crash?"

When Denny mentioned the name Carlton O'Bannion, Barker's face darkened immediately, a veil of definite anger covering it.

"I know O'Bannion, personally and by reputation. If you'll allow me, I'll take care of any business left between you. I have the feeling if you go there yourself, I might have to wait a while to put you to work." Barker gave a tight little smile.

"A definite possibility, Mr. Barker. If it wouldn't be inconvenient, I'd appreciate that. I generally like to take care of my own business, though I'd rather not see the man again. In all likelihood, it would get bad."

"Done then. Think no more about it. Do you have a place to stay until I can get you on the job?"

"I'll find something, not a problem."

"Nonsense," Caroline spoke firmly. "Daddy has a huge old place. I'm sure he could put you up, right Dad?"

"If I had been given a chance, daughter, I was going to make the offer. That way Denny, I could fill you in on what you'd have to do on the job, and I could tell you about the projects we have planned. You might find it interesting."

"And I'll be coming home tomorrow," Caroline said. "So we can visit when daddy's not filling your head with logistics. I want to know more about your life, if you wouldn't get annoyed with all my questions."

"Not at all," Denny replied, giving her a direct look.

At that moment, the door opened and a young man came in and went right over to Caroline, and bent down and kissed her. With his hand on her shoulder he said, "Sorry I couldn't get here sooner, C, are you okay?"

She smiled at him and nodded slightly. "Denny, this is my fiancé, Chad. Chad, this is the man who rescued me from the plane crash, Denny Caraway."

Chad turned and grabbed Denny by the hand, pumping it vigorously. "Thank you so much for what you've done, Mr. Caraway. I don't know what would become of me if I'd lost her."

Looking at the man for a long moment, Denny nodded.

Quick to size up the situation, and noticing the look on Denny's face, Barker said, "Come on, Denny, let's go get a drink. After the last few days, you could probably use one."

Denny picked up on Nathan Barker's suggestion as a way out of an awkward situation and appreciated the gesture. "That's one offer I won't turn down, Mr. Barker, thanks."

"Call me Nathan, please."

After having a couple of shots of good bourbon along with a tasty steak dinner at a nearby restaurant, Barker took Denny to his truck and led the way over to the Barker residence, located on Chena Ridge. It was a huge log home, like nothing he'd ever been in before — downright majestic. The lower outside walls were natural river stones and the logs of the upper walls were large. The inside was expansive, with high beamed ceilings, natural wood stairways and railings, and large windows, giving a terrific view of the surrounding country. Clearly, a lot of thought had gone into the place. Though it had been built on a grand scale, it had a warm rustic quality. Denny wasn't surprised to learn Barker had designed and built it himself. It turned out the man was also an architect.

Nathan gave Denny the tour, which included a large game room literally filled with mounts of animals from many different countries. Nathan was obviously a world class hunter. Caraway was curious, because there was no grizzly or brown bear in the collection. When he asked Barker why, Barker gave a funny little smile. "I've had several opportunities to take a trophy class brownie, but when I got the animals in my scope, for some reason, I couldn't shoot them. I can't really explain it, I just can't take a big bear. Can you understand?"

"Well, I have no problems with trophy hunting, Nathan, even though all the animals I've taken have been for food or to defend myself. I don't think I could shoot a big bear either. To me, they symbolize everything wild and larger than life about Alaska. Shooting one for sport wouldn't set right with me."

"I see your point, and I'll think on it," Barker said. "I noticed your old model 70 Winchester. What caliber is it?"

When Caraway told him it was a 30-06, Barker suggested Denny get himself a heavier caliber for work. "I'm sure you can shoot your rifle well. Still, I would feel better if you had a gun in a heavier caliber, as a more reliable stopper on big bears. I'll be happy to foot the bill for it." Denny thought for a moment and agreed there was wisdom in the idea.

"Come on then, I'll show you to your room. Big day tomorrow, Caroline coming home and all. Have you noticed she's a high energy person? Give her a chance and she'll wear you out." Nathan Barker gave Denny a searching look.

The question in Nathan's eyes was obvious. Denny thought for a moment and replied, "I've only known your daughter a short time and in an unusual situation. I will tell you I think she has a great personality. Chad's a lucky guy. A man would be a fool not to appreciate her qualities."

Barker smiled and said, "Can't fault a man for having good judgment. She and Chad have been friends since childhood. They've decided to tie the knot next April. He's a good man, an accountant here in Fairbanks. It's late, let's get some rest."

Caroline came home the next day and Nathan was right. Whenever he and Denny weren't discussing Denny's upcoming job or business in general, Caroline was pumping him for information about his homesteading life and all his experiences. Denny hadn't talked so much in years. At one point he laughed and told her she ought to write a book. She smiled and told him if he'd let her, she would — about him. Denny smiled and shook his head, saying, "No, thanks, I'd rather keep things private, though I appreciate your suggestion." She was visibly disappointed, but let it drop.

Three days later, Nathan told Denny he was going to Anchorage on business, and asked him to come along. Grateful for a change and a little breathing room, he agreed.

In the morning, they drove out to Fairbanks International Airport and parked in a light aircraft area. Barker was an experienced pilot and owned a pristine 1956 de Havilland Beaver, a Canadian-made bush plane with a great reputation for reliability. Though Caraway had seen them, he'd never flown in one.

"She's a fine aircraft," Nathan said, "extremely reliable, with a large cargo capacity. I've had her in and out of some tight spots, and this plane has never let me down. Let's get buckled in."

In minutes, they were flying smoothly along, the Beaver reminding Denny of a giant mechanical bumblebee. The big radial engine was putting out plenty of noise, making it necessary to wear headsets to be able to talk. The two men discussed the airplane's character, the country they were flying over, and many things Alaskan.

Denny settled into a silent observation of the terrain below. In all the years he had been in the state, his enthusiasm and love for it had never diminished. To him, Alaska had its own autonomy, a natural independence unlike anywhere else Caraway had been. It was far beyond any other state's natural dynamics. No matter what happened, life in Alaska always seemed wider and fuller.

All too quickly, they were coming into the Anchorage airport. Nathan had a work truck parked by his hangar, and Denny, while waiting for Nathan to finish his conversation with a man from Barker Surveying, had a cup of the most potent coffee he'd ever drunk. He figured the pot must have been heating all day in the hangar office, and Caraway figured he could float a quarter on top. Still, he finished the cup.

Afterwards, Nathan and Denny went over to several supply houses to pick up specially ordered surveying equipment and other supplies.

With all the needed supplies in the truck, they drove over to a well-known gun store, Great Northern Guns, which had been in business for many years. When they went in, Nathan walked over to talk to the owner, Joe, who he'd apparently known for a long time, judging by the way they greeted each other, interacting as only friends bonded by meaningful experiences can. While standing there listening, Denny noticed one photo among many, displayed up on a wall. In it, was Joe, Nathan, and one other fellow standing by a huge bull moose one of them had taken. It was a massive animal with a gigantic set of antlers. The scene appeared to be typical willow country somewhere in

Alaska, and the men looked as though they'd been hunting for a while. The photo spoke volumes about the connection these sportsmen shared.

Someone said, "What can I do for you, sir?" Denny turned to see a very large man sitting behind a glass-topped counter, under which were several shelves full of semi-auto pistols. He was obviously ready to give Denny his undivided attention.

"I need a suitable rifle for shooting big bears."

"Have you been around big bears much? They do demand a large bore rifle."

Denny responded with a facetious remark, unusual for him when confronted with a stranger. "I didn't know bears shot rifles."

The big man stared at him for a minute, and said, "If you're really interested in buying a gun, I'll be glad to help you."

Smiling to himself, Denny nodded and the salesman showed him several guns, all fancy grade magnums, large caliber rifles, one of which was an engraved European model.

Denny told him he wanted a good basic working gun, maybe a 375 H&H, but nothing too fancy.

The man seemed a little disappointed that Caraway didn't want the top grade guns he had shown him, pointed to a rack of used firearms, and told Denny he could look at the rifles there. Finding one 375 H&H, he brought the gun back to the counter. It had obviously been on a few hunts, but looked solid enough, a bolt action with a low-power variable scope on it. Though Denny had always used open sights with his Winchester, he liked the fast way this gun and scope lined up on a target. The various small scratches and dents on the stock didn't bother him.

The salesman said, "This one isn't the quality of the other ones I've shown you; however, it's solid and will probably do the job for you. We have plenty of 375 ammunition in stock."

Denny told the man he'd take it, with three boxes of ammunition, which he picked out from the many boxes on a shelf.

As the man was writing up the necessary paperwork, Nathan came over and said, smiling, "Hello, Yog, scare off any obnoxious customers lately?"

Denny said, "Yog?"

With a glint in his eye, Yog said, "Yes, sir, if that's okay with you."

"Well, if it's okay with you, then there's not much I can say about it. A man's name is his own business."

"That is true. I have to do the background check to finish the transaction. Only take a few minutes."

Nathan took out his checkbook and asked Yog for the full amount.

Yog asked, "Is this gun for you or for this man?"

"This man is going to work for me as a bear guard, Yog, and I'm buying the gun for him to use for that purpose, but it is a piece of equipment for my company. I asked him to pick out a good one."

"Well, if that's the case, there's no problem whatsoever."

Nathan filled out the necessary paperwork and handed him a check for the purchase.

Getting everything in order, Yog told him, "I just need to do the background check and we'll be all set."

The background check cleared and the deal was done.

As they were leaving, Denny stuck out his hand. Without hesitation, Yog shook it. Denny was aware of the great strength in the big man's arm, though Yog didn't exert any undue force.

"Thanks for buying your rifle here, sir, I appreciate it."

Nathan and Denny headed back to the airport after having a mid-day breakfast at Gwennie's, a long-established restaurant with lots of antiques and other items relating to life in Alaska, including an old full mount grizzly bear which had seen better days, judging from its hairless patches and moth-eaten ears.

On the way to the airport. Nathan mentioned, "Yog takes a little getting used to, but he certainly knows guns."

"Oh," said Denny, "I've met worse."

The two men returned to the Chena Ridge house that evening, after unloading the new gear from the Beaver at the Barker Surveying Company warehouse. The next day, Nathan took Denny out to the local shooting range to sight in the gun. Though it had a lot more recoil than the 30-06, Denny found it comfortable enough to shoot accurately, and it took only a half box of ammo to get it sighted right in at 100 yards.

Nathan told him, "You can shoot to point of aim from 0 to 200 yards with that cartridge, Denny, handy in the bush, as you certainly know."

Denny nodded his agreement.

Two days later, Denny was out with a crew working some remote land on a BLM contract in an area called the Farewell Burn, about forty miles from the village of Nikolai. A parcel of the burn, first surveyed in the mid eighties, needed to be redone, and Barker had taken the contract.

It was a bleak area, having gained its name from a huge fire in 1978, Alaska's largest forest fire on record. The surveying crew flew to the little town of McGrath, then to a strip at the burn itself.

Some trees were coming back, though it was covered mostly with willows and grasses. It was obvious to Denny the place had been totally devastated. It wasn't nice country, but that didn't matter. He was there to do a job.

There were some bears around as the crew worked the survey, though none of them came close enough to be a worry. Once in a while, one of them would let out a roar. One of the newer guys on the crew looked concerned the first time it happened, but Denny told him not to worry. "He's just letting us know he's aware of us." The new guy gave a half-hearted smile and went back to work, looking around occasionally while he worked.

A problem did occur when a huge American Bison bull came into camp and caused a disturbance. Denny knew there were transplanted bison in the area, there to be hunted. To see one in the Alaska bush instead of out on the Midwestern plains seemed a little strange to him.

The massive old bull came into camp one morning and stayed for over an hour, threatening crew members and causing some general confusion. Denny stayed on alert, keeping a reasonable distance from the bull, yet close enough to make a good shot if necessary. Though there were several moments when Caraway thought he might have to put the beast down, fortunately it wasn't necessary, and the bison finally wandered off.

The only time Denny had any real trouble was when one of the crew, after the work day was over, decided to do a little exploring on his own, unarmed. Denny caught up with him and asked him to come back to camp.

The guy got huffy, grumbling that he had lived in Alaska for years, and didn't need a baby sitter.

Caraway gave him one of his long looks and told the belligerent man he had a job to do and didn't plan on letting him make it any more difficult than necessary. "I don't give a damn what you do, or what happens on your own time, but I was hired to keep everybody safe, and that's what I intend to do. Let's go."

The guy tried to stare Denny down, glaring at him, until, when he finally realized he was dealing with a man of resolute character, turned and walked back to camp. There was no trouble from him after that.

Denny handled his job with ease, traveling around to various remote sites with the crews, and several right on the outskirts of Anchorage and Fairbanks, sometimes just standing around, keeping watch with the rifle resting easily on his shoulder. Occasionally, he had a little time to explore the areas they were working in, never straying too far from the camp however, in case something came up. He got along with the crew well enough; though, as is often the case, there was one wise guy, always making remarks, who Denny found mildly irritating, as did the rest of the crew. The man was a good surveyor, so he was tolerated.

At one job, working on a piece of land by a major river the state was developing for a public camping site, Nathan Barker came cruising up on an airboat. He got out, tied the boat off and walked right up to where Denny was standing. Nathan smiled and handed Denny an envelope. It contained a check for twenty-five hundred dollars. Denny gave Barker a questioning look.

"Denny, I went down and had a little chat with Carlton a few days ago. He and I have had a few encounters in the past. I convinced him to make out your check, and told him you deserved a bonus for the extra work you had done for him, to which he agreed."

"This is almost twice as much as I was supposed to get."

"True, and O'Bannion had made out a check for less, which he insisted was all you were owed, until I told him you were still working when you were forced to undertake an unnecessary and dangerous wilderness hike back to civilization. He put up a bit of a fuss, and let's just say I know more about the S.O.B. than he realized, and he finally saw the wisdom in taking my advice. So, enjoy the bonus; you deserve it. Besides, I liked seeing his face turn as red as his beard." Nathan broke out a big grin.

Shaking Denny's hand, he went to talk to the crew chief about the way the job was going, then walked back to his airboat, cranked it up, and headed down river.

Chapter Twenty

It was mid October and temperatures were rapidly dropping. They'd had several light snows, and work was becoming more difficult to complete. On November First, a real snow hit in the area northeast of Tok where they were located. When the storm abated, it was time to break camp and get hauled out with all their gear. Nathan made a couple of hops in the Beaver to help out with the camp break-down. Denny's work for the season was over. He spent several days helping Nathan get things sorted out back in Fairbanks, enjoying the accomplished man's company.

None too soon, Denny was free to head home to Lanyard Creek. He had been ready for quite a while. Though it was good to make some money, and Nathan gave him a bonus for his work, he needed to get back to the peace and solitude of the homestead, or at least he thought so.

Denny's life would be back on a seasonally defined schedule. He was glad to be off the clock, though he had been offered the same position next summer, and gladly agreed. Before leaving Fairbanks, he'd given Nathan detailed instructions on how to get to his place, when Barker suggested he come see him later that winter. Denny hoped he would have time to come out for a visit.

Caraway Checked in at the post office when he first reached Salcha, and the postmaster gave him a cardboard box filled mostly with trash mail. Denny found it amusing that he got so many catalogues in the mail, living as he did.

When Denny got back to his trailer, he found that Elliot had kept the place ready for him, plowing the snow, sweeping the front steps off, and making sure the heater was running right. He'd have to bring him some fresh moose meat when he was able.

Caraway figured he was going to have an interesting ride in on the winter trail. He had, of necessity, ridden his ATV out to Salcha at the beginning of summer to find work. Now, he would have to take it back in over the snow-covered trail. There hadn't been any heavy snowfalls yet, judging from the snow he'd seen, but the amount of snow in Salcha was only a general indicator of what he might find down the trail.

After Denny had settled into the trailer for the night, he went through his mail, tossing most of it into the trash. But there was one personal letter, from Gwen O'Mara. Denny paused for a moment, before opening the envelope, thinking back to the last time he had been with her. Inside was a newspaper clipping from the Hazel Trumpeter dated August 29th, 2000, and a brief note.

The newspaper article read:

A Hazel man was fatally shot by his wife at their homestead on Long Bay. The incident was reported by a neighbor who came upon the scene shortly after it had occurred. When questioned by state troopers, the wife said, "I just couldn't take any more of him. There'll be a whole lot of people a whole lot better off now."

The woman, Laura Waters, alternately laughed and cried during questioning. She had bruises and other signs of possible physical abuse. Her husband, Bucky Waters, was a long time homesteader, his land located northeast of the head of Long Bay.

When asked what he thought, Waters' homesteading neighbor who had reported the incident said, "Well, I'm not really all that surprised. There were a number people who didn't care much for Bucky. I guess his wife turned out to be one of them."

There are no plans for a memorial service at this time.

After reading the article, Denny considered the news it held. It wasn't totally unexpected. He'd assumed someone would eventually take care of Waters, and was glad he didn't have to bother, but felt bad for Bucky's wife, hoping she wouldn't be charged for what was, in his mind, a favor to humanity.

Folding up the article and putting it in his pack, he read the simple little note Gwen had included. All it said was, "I miss you. Gwen"

Tucking the note away with the newspaper article, Denny laid out all his gear. It was a wise move on his part to keep a set of winter clothes and gear at the trailer. He had never had to use it before, but this situation would change that fact. The ATV started easily in the cold dark morning hour when Denny made ready to head home. He had bought a few items in Fairbanks to replace the perishables he had taken from the cabin and given Elliot the previous

June. They made a simple load on the wheeler's racks, along with his chainsaw and emergency supplies.

Dressed for the run, including a ski mask to protect his face, Denny rode down to the trail head at the Salcha river recreational area and headed home.

The trail was rough going from the beginning. Denny had never run his wheeler in real winter conditions, always having a snow machine for that. There was enough snow to make it necessary for the wheeler to go plowing through the cold white stuff, forcing the snow off to the sides like the bow of a boat through water. In some spots, the ATV began high centering on the snow being forced under it, and Caraway had to stand on the footrests and rock back and forth to keep it from floundering.

Denny had been right to think there might be more snow farther out the trail. The snow was deep in some areas, and he had to walk in front of the wheeler on the aluminum bear paw snowshoes he had kept at the trailer to break trail for his struggling machine. By the time he reached the bridge he had built over the little creek, he was exhausted, after spending over ten hours on the trail already. Denny needed a break, so he ran the wheeler over the bridge to a spot close beyond that would do for a quick camp. He cleared the ground close under a large spruce tree, and got a small fire going. The clothes he wore under the parka were damp with sweat from his exertions, and he took them off to replace with the set in his pack.

Caraway sat by the little fire, the layer of cut spruce branches keeping him off the cold ground. He didn't grumble to himself about the situation. No sense in doing that. He chewed on a licorice whip, ate a little clean snow, and rested. Hungry later, Denny opened one of the packs of bacon he had bought, strung half a dozen strips on a willow stick, and hung them close to the fire to cook.

The forest was quiet, sound muffled by the snow covering the trees and ground. Denny let his mind drift, listening to the sound of the fire, accentuated by the sizzling strips of cooking bacon. The smell of it was making his stomach growl. Pulling one piece off the willow branch, he sat contentedly chewing. It wasn't as filling as his moose jerky, but would do for now. It didn't take long for him to finish all the bacon, lick his fingers clean, load up the wheeler, and continue on.

The rest of the trail was easier going because he had done more clearing on the stretches closer to the cabin, so that there were fewer low bushes hidden in the snow to make for tough riding. Still it wasn't easy, but Caraway could feel how close he was to his homestead, and that kept him going.

It was now about a mile to his cabin. Denny had been running with his headlights on in the winter darkness. Riding an easy piece of trail that was located between Lanyard Creek on the right and an area of deep forest on the left, Denny stopped because the headlights had lit up a big bull moose walking down the trail towards him. The lights gave the massive animal an eerie appearance. The old bull still had his rack, and though he was past his prime, it was impressive. The moose stopped a short distance away and stood staring at Denny, probably wondering why the curious critter before him didn't have the sense to get out of its way.

Denny shut the engine off. He spoke calmly but clearly to the moose, letting him know there was nothing to be bothered about, but there was really no way, at that point, Denny could ride around the moose, or the moose walk around the ATV.

Caraway knew what would come next and he didn't have long to wait. The moose thumped the ground twice with a front hoof, lowered its head and began rocking his antlers back and forth. Denny slipped off the wheeler and waited.

Sure enough, the bull made a quick little charge right at the wheeler and Denny ran into the trees, half hiding behind a big spruce to watch the moose.

Now directly in front of the ATV, the moose blew a heavy cloud of breath from its ponderous muzzle and thumped the front rack with its hoof, making a loud metallic sound. The noise spooked the moose and it pivoted to the right, and glided into the trees, away from Denny.

Caraway waited several minutes, then walked over to the ATV. The front rack where the moose had struck it had a definite dent in the tubular metal, but no other damage. Restarting the engine, he continued on his way, watching the trees for the cantankerous old bull.

Half an hour later, he arrived at his homestead. As was always his way, he sat for a minute on the machine, glad for a safe arrival home.

The log cabin and the old plywood cabin he used now for storage both looked to be in good shape, though there appeared to be several tufts of bear fur snagged on nails sticking out of the bear boards.

Opening the door to the cabin, Caraway saw his home was as he had left it, though there were some vole droppings on the floor, and later he found an old nest in some paper and rags gathered together under the bed, now deserted.

When he started a fire in the wood stove, the cabin immediately filled with smoke. He had forgotten to remove the coffee can from over the top of the stove pipe. Putting a ladder against an eave, he climbed up and rectified the situation, then waited a few minutes for the smoke to clear.

Sitting by the now crackling fire showing through the open stove door, the supplies stashed away, his feet up by the fire, a cup of hot tea in hand, Denny thought to himself, "You've been away from home too long."

That night, he thought of Gwen as he dozed off to sleep. He was caught in a quandary. Denny had turned fifty-one while working for O'Bannion. As much as he loved being back on the homestead, he felt as if things were not the same for him there, and he knew what it was. For the first time in all his years homesteading, he was beginning to feel the pangs of loneliness. He had never given being alone any thought before. Now, he wasn't sure what to do. He'd be damned if he'd give up the homestead, no matter what. Being with other people the past few months had been a mixture of accepting and often enjoying human company, and annoyance at not being able to have his long-accepted peace and solitude.

Though glad to get the newspaper clipping and the abrupt note from Gwen, he half wished she hadn't communicated at all. It had stirred his emotions, which were usually neatly wrapped up and stored away. Even so, once he was settled in his own bed, Denny slept better than he had in months.

Over the following weeks, he busied himself with the chores of living the homestead life. Firewood was in low supply, as working all summer had put him behind, so he began cutting and splitting right after arriving back home. He did have some wood leftover, stacked, and seasoned. As an experienced homesteader, he always cut more than he anticipated needing and cut more during the winter, when hauling by snow machine and sled was possible. Though he had been cutting wood for years, and had to travel a little farther to find good trees, he had a whole forest to choose from, and within a month he was well supplied, for the rest of the winter season.

Denny had a special place by the edge of the creek close behind his cabin which he used for gathering water all year round. He had cleared stones and deepened a nice pool, building a small wooden platform to stand or kneel on to fill his buckets. If the winter got extra cold, he'd have to move farther out because the water by the bank would freeze solid. Simply a fact of life there on Lanyard Creek.

Three days after getting home, he took time to go out and take a moose for winter meat. It was the easiest hunt he'd ever been on. He walked about one hundred yards down the back trail and there, standing broadside to the trail, was an older cow moose. He watched for a while to check for a young moose with her, but she was alone, barren. The moose never even moved from where she stood stripping willow leaves off a now sorry-looking bush. Denny took careful aim and made a clean head shot. The moose went down instantly, never knowing what hit her.

Now there was meat. Field dressing and quartering the animal was much harder than the hunt itself. So close to home, Caraway didn't need the snow machine and sled. He simply picked up the quarters, ribs and other bits and carried them to the hanging rack next to his cabin. He spent the next day butchering the meat, packing it into the cache and moving the gut pile, hide, and unusable parts a good distance from his home.

The supplies Denny had brought in included the treats he liked to have around: licorice whips, chocolate chip cookies, and peanut butter. When the day's work was over and he could relax in the cabin, he often enjoyed a cup of coffee, perhaps a good book, and a stack of cookies on the table.

He had put the disappointment of Caroline Barker being unavailable out of his mind, helped somewhat by the note from Gwen. Upon reflection, it was the brief intimate connection with Caroline that had put certain things in perspective.

Chapter Twenty One

After two months back on his land, Denny decided to head into town. He felt an urge to go to the North Star Cafe for the burger he had intended to enjoy when he first got back to Salcha. Denny loaded up the snow machine with his trail gear and headed out to the highway. The weather had gotten quite cold — well below zero, and there had been several heavy snowfalls which had settled and compacted, so the trail surface was good. Already stocked up with major supplies, he left the sled behind. The few things he'd pick up in Salcha could go in the snow machine's rear rack. This was the first time Denny had gone to town on a whim, rather than out of necessity.

Denny left home in the dark and arrived at the North Star Cafe in the dark, though it was barely four-thirty in the afternoon. Charlie Brady, as always, was ready with his coffee when Caraway walked in.

"Mr. Caraway," Brady said.

"Officer Brady," Denny responded.

"Haven't seen you in a while. How have things been?"

"Been working out of Fairbanks. Bear guards aren't in high demand during the winter, so season's over. It was a good job, though it got a little crowded with the crew and all."

"Anything more than two people can be a bit much, right?"

"That's right Charlie. How about one of your good burgers. I've been wanting one for a while."

"Coming right up. With everything, right?"

"That's the way I like it, with fries, and don't forget the ketchup."

As Denny ate, he regaled Charlie Brady with his experiences working with Carlton O'Bannion, and how it had ended.

Denny noticed a change in Brady's face at the mention of O'Bannion. He knew Brady'd had a long career as an Alaska State Trooper working wildlife situations and wondered if he and O'Bannion had crossed paths. Turned out he was right.

"Denny, I wish you could have somehow let me know you'd be working for the man. I would have warned you off. Think I'll get in touch with one of my old trooper buddies still on the job and have him check up on the guy, just to keep him on his toes."

"Fine with me, Charlie. Do what you think is best."

It had been a long day on the trail, so Caraway told Brady good night and headed down to his trailer on the snow machine to spend the night. He had decided to go into Anchorage early the next morning to get a new chainsaw. Though the one he had was good quality, ten years on the job had worn it out. He found he couldn't get the one he wanted in Fairbanks when he got the rest of his supplies. He wished his old friend Ed from Hazel was still around, because he trusted Gundross and could depend on him. But, Ed was gone now. He wondered if his saw shop was still open, with a new owner.

Denny hadn't planned on doing what he did; he was merely responding to subconscious urges. In Anchorage, he stopped at one chainsaw dealer, picked up a new saw that was the same model as the one he had worn out, paid for it, and was back on the road in fifteen minutes, only stopping one more time to gas up, then continuing south until he reached Hazel. Though he liked the journey down the highway to the little coastal town, he didn't pay as much attention to the scenery as he might have if he didn't have something else on his mind. By the time Denny reached Hazel, he had come to a decision about where he wanted his life to go. He went right over to the Log Cabin Cafe and parked, sitting in the truck until he saw Gwen through the window, coffee pot in hand.

He took a deep breath, got out of his truck, and went into the cafe. Gwen was cleaning off a table, and she looked up as Denny reached her. Taking her in his arms, he gave her a long, serious kiss. She didn't resist, and when they stopped, several customers were chuckling in the background. He smiled a full smile at her and said, "I've missed you too."

Later that night, having made up for much lost time, they lay snuggled together, talking quietly.

"So, Mr. Caraway, did you get what you came for?"

"I really didn't know what to expect, but I had to come back and find out. Sad news about Bucky." There was a definite lack of sincerity in his voice.

"Not to my way of thinking, Denny. So, what are your plans? Still have your homestead up north?"

She gently touched one of the three scars on his upper left arm, a permanent reminder of the dangers of living in the deep bush. When she'd asked him what had happened, seeing the scars for the first time, he told her he'd had a difference of opinion with an old, hungry winter bear.

"He wanted to have me for dinner and I refused the invitation." He had given one of his little half smiles then, but Gwen didn't smile back.

"Of course, Gwen; I have no plans to leave it. Did that once before."

"I recall. You probably wouldn't want anyone else out there, would you, being a solitary man."

Denny's gut got tight when Gwen spoke, but all he said was, "Something on your mind, Gwen?"

She took a little breath, then said, "There's not much here for me in Hazel. A lot of the people I knew are gone, I don't like the ones living here now, and as I said in the note, dammit, I've missed you. You got under my skin, Mr. Caraway, and it turns out there's nothing I can do about it. It's pretty obvious to me you still enjoy my company, so what would you think about having me as a homesteading partner. Do you think you'd have room for me? I know how to split wood, dress out a moose, and haul water, as you well know. I'm more than willing to give it a try if you are. Besides, I've got a good snow machine and sled for hauling, my dad's old rifle, and plenty of cold weather gear, so you'd be getting a complete package deal."

"I don't know, Gwen, can you cook?"

Gwen began giving him a flurry of small punches in the ribs, until he grabbed her arms, pulled her against him and, looking directly into her eyes with an intensity that made her go limp in his arms, said, "Gwen, I wouldn't have it any other way. Let's sleep on it, see how it feels in the morning."

"I won't feel any different in the morning Denny, and besides, I don't feel like sleeping."

Denny decided he wasn't sleepy yet either.

Denny woke up to the smell of fresh coffee and the sound of bacon sizzling in a skillet. Stretching and yawning, feeling relaxed and content, he got up and went into the kitchen. Walking up behind Gwen, busy at the stove, he grabbed her around the waist and kissed her neck. He felt a little thrill run through her.

Without turning around she said, "You better put something on, so you don't get splattered with hot grease somewhere you'll regret."

"How do you know I'm not dressed already?"

"Oh, I can tell, Mr. Caraway."

He smiled and walked into the bathroom to wash up.

Over breakfast, Denny and Gwen discussed the details of her move to Lanyard Creek. They never asked each other if they were sure, because there was no doubt in either of their minds this was the right thing.

It took two weeks to sort out and pack up everything she would be taking, and it was going to take several trips to the homestead to get everything out there. Winter was the best time for freighting, and would make the task easier.

Gwen wasn't kidding when she said she had plenty of cold weather gear. She had hats, including a fine beaver skin trapper hat, gloves and mitts, a Carhartt arctic lined set of coveralls with a hood, a down parka, wool pants, insulated pacs, and more.

Her dad's old rifle really was a beaut. A collector would have given his eye teeth for it. It was a Winchester model 71, the last version of the model 1886. It was a special piece though, because it had been reworked by Harold Johnson, a famous gunsmith from Coopers Landing, Alaska, who had rechambered it for his .450 Alaskan cartridge, as was stamped on the barrel. It was capable of bringing down the biggest animal in Alaska, the brown bear. Denny wondered if she could handle such a powerful round but was wise enough not to say anything, figuring he would eventually find out.

Gwen had considered selling her parents' old cabin before Denny showed up. Now she went down to a friend's realty office, and asked her to get the selling process started while she and Denny got things cleared out. Rhoda, the realtor, assured her it would be an easy sell, at a price that surprised Gwen. She had no idea the property was worth so much.

Finally, they got things all set for their journey north. Gwen had a four-foot by eight-foot utility trailer to tow behind Denny's truck. She told him whatever wouldn't fit in there or in his truck wasn't going. She donated a lot to the Hazel thrift store, and gave some things away to people she knew, including a few electric kitchen appliances she'd have no further use for. She looked forward to living the homestead life, remembering the way things were when she was a kid. Her parents gave up their simple life slowly, modernizing only when it seemed beneficial and a better way to live. They hadn't had indoor plumbing in the family home until her dad had died and Gwen insisted on it. Now, using an outhouse again sounded just fine. Gwen wondered if Denny used a seat of hard foam insulation to keep from getting frostbite of the butt in winter. The foam almost instantly warmed when you sat down in the privy even when it was thirty below outside.

Rhoda had potential buyers before they left Hazel, retired folks who had come up from the Lower 48 the previous spring to visit in a huge RV and decided to stay. They didn't even argue the price. So, things were on track. All the necessary preparations falling so easily into place seemed to affirm they were on the right path.

Three weeks from the day he arrived in Hazel, Denny drove his truck onto the trailer's driveway in Salcha with Gwen beside him. It had been a busy time for them both, so loading the sleds could wait until morning.

The propane heater was running on low, and the trailer was chilly, and Denny turned it up. They were hungry, so the two of them drove over to the North Star Cafe for a meal. When Charlie Brady looked up and saw Denny walk in with Gwen, he was caught off guard, never having seen Denny arrive with anyone else, much less a woman.

Gwen walked up to him, stuck out her hand and said, "Hi, I'm Gwen O'Mara, and you must be Officer Brady."

Charlie gave Denny a fake scowl, then smiled at Gwen and told her to call him Charlie. He looked at Denny and said, "You sly dog, you. What did you do, go to the university and take up with a co-ed?"

"Enough of that, Charlie," Gwen remarked, a little smile on her face. Changing the subject, she said, "This is a nice eatery you have here, how about a tour of the facilities?"

"Oh, it's not very interesting to see."

"It is to me. I know my way around a cafe, believe you me."

Charlie poured Denny a cup, told him to sit, and took Gwen into the kitchen. Denny heard them chuckle a few times, and wondered if it was the kitchen they were discussing.

"Can a man get a meal around here?" He yelled at the two of them still conversing in the kitchen.

"Hold your horses, Mr. Caraway," Gwen yelled back. "We're talking professionally over here!" Soon enough, Denny heard the sounds and smells of cooking coming from the kitchen. He was glad there were no other customers in the place, making the little get-together possible and more enjoyable.

After a while though, Denny became antsy to get out to Lanyard Creek with Gwen, to watch her reactions to the homestead. He had a feeling she would love it. He knew Gwen would be a good partner. Only time would tell how good.

The three of them sat down to a dinner of halibut and chips, after Charlie had put the closed sign up and shut off the outside lights. This, he knew, was a special time, and he enjoyed being part of it. His opinion of Denny Caraway had actually gone up, though he already had plenty of respect for the man. Now, he had more because Denny was willing to commit to something with this gal that would change both their lives, no matter the outcome. Charlie had known a number of homesteaders in his time, some of them real old sourdoughs who had resided way out in the bush for many years. Most of them were a "little off" in his opinion, and he knew it was from living alone for so long. He'd already decided Denny had gone a little feral and wondered how far that would go. But now things had changed. This new development for him could only be a good thing.

The next morning Denny and Gwen loaded up the sleds and headed out the trail. Gwen proved to be a good trail rider, keeping up with Denny as he pushed along. Gwen's sled was big enough to haul a fair load. Another trip with this sled and Denny's big aluminum rig, and one more with his sled alone would probably do it. Denny had a good eye for such things, and Gwen knew how to pack. In fact, they worked smoothly together as if they had done so for years, helping each other to get the job done. Watching her carefully packing a box with some fragile keepsakes, Denny got a little lump in his throat. He still hadn't grown accustomed to being with her in this way, but he liked it a lot. When she turned and saw him giving her a look she hadn't seen on him before, she gave him an inquiring little lift of her chin, and he smiled at her. "Just like bread and butter," he thought.

Denny didn't ride quite as fast as he usually did, to spare Gwen any excess roughness. When they stopped about halfway to check the loads, she told him if he wanted to go a little faster, it was okay. "I'm enjoying this trail; it's smoother than some I've been on." Denny smiled and gave her cold nose a kiss and they continued on, a little faster.

By four in the afternoon, they arrived at Denny's homestead, the new cabin right in front of them. They both sat there a moment, enjoying their arrival.

"Denny, it's a beautiful cabin, even better than I expected when you told me about it. You've made a good life here. I feel I've come home, somehow."

"Because you have, Gwen." Gwen got off her machine and jumped on Denny, hugging and kissing him with pure joy. Whether he knew it or not, he had given her a new lease on life. She had given up expecting much, and this was better than she could have imagined.

They went inside, Gwen starting a fire in the woodstove to warm the cold cabin, while Denny started bringing things in, stacking them out of the way until they could sort everything out. The two of them sat at the spruce table in their outdoor clothing until the cabin warmed up.

Gwen insisted on making eggs and bacon for dinner, though Denny wanted to do the cooking. He sat watching her bustle about, finding everything she needed. Though it was a simple meal, the two of them were well aware it was their first one together on the homestead, and that made it special.

Though they were beat from the long day, the two of them had trouble dropping off, talking quietly until sleep finally overtook the both of them. The last thing Denny heard Gwen say was, "We're going to need a bigger bed."

The next morning and what occurred then became the traditional start of a day for Denny and Gwen. Though he was an early riser, she was always up before him, stoking the fire, getting coffee fixings together, and when the stove was hot enough she'd get a good breakfast going. Denny would awaken to those great morning smells, put on his boots and jacket to answer nature's call, then come in to a hot mug of joe waiting at the table. Though Gwen never knew it, Denny would sometimes watch her from bed as she bustled around the cabin, pretending to be asleep if she looked his way.

She wasn't sure when Denny began saying it, until one morning she realized he always said, "Morning, love." It had been such a natural sounding greeting that it slipped right by her. She, in her wry way said, "Morning Mr. Caraway." Denny loved her saying that, as much as a more affectionate reply. It was Gwen speaking in her own way.

The first time Denny brought in an armload of firewood to put in the wood box by the fireplace, Gwen went right out after him and brought in another. When he went out to clear some freshly-fallen snow from around the cabin, she had a basin of water waiting to warm his hands and face when he came back in. Though the two had feelings for each other already, being alone in the bush away from outside influences that could alter their relationship drew them closer day by day. They complemented each other in nearly every way, and the old saw about two people becoming one, growing into each other, was no truer than with these two.

The rest of their first winter together smoothly slipped along. The temperatures dropped down to forty below several times, but they were warm and snug in the log cabin. They were forced to stay in during a few blizzards lasting several days, and did little indoor chores such as repairing clothing and cleaning gear, playing card games or dominoes, and drinking the mixture of coffee and cocoa Denny had begun drinking during his first year on his old homestead. Gwen was a little leery of such a mixture, but once she tried it, she was hooked. All in all, life was sweet. When the storms passed, they both went out and cleared away the snow, freed the snow machines from winter's frozen grip, and kept the homestead going.

Chapter Twenty Two

Supplies begun running out faster than Denny had anticipated with the two of them there on the homestead. When he had lived alone, he would often miss a meal, busy working on his chores and projects. Gwen made sure he was well feed, which also meant, when he was enjoying one of her well-cooked meals, she got to spend more time with him.

So, in early February, with the cold holding at twenty below, a light snow drifting down, they bundled up in clothing of wool and down and headed out to the highway, using both snow machines, with the big sled attached to Denny's rig. When they got to the trailer in Salcha, old Elliot was shoveling snow from the driveway and front porch steps, while his grandson Drew shoveled the roof. The old man had been really wonderful about caring for Denny's place when he was out on the 'stead, asking nothing in return. Of course, Caraway always found a way to make it right with him, often bringing him some game meat or buying him beer at the Salcha grocery.

Gwen gave Elliot a hug, thanking him for being so sweet. With a self-conscious smile, he said, "Oh, I'm just an old man with time on my hands. It gives me something to do." Denny smiled at Elliot's offhand way of making it seem as if they were doing him a favor.

As with Charlie Brady, Elliot had been surprised to see Caraway with a woman by his side. Smiling broadly, he said, "How in the world did a crusty old homesteader like you get himself such a nice lady to take care of him?"

Gwen immediately replied, "He just wore me down with begging and pleading. I felt so sorry for him, I finally gave in."

Denny silently shook his head slowly back and forth, a twinkle in his eye.

Warming up the truck the next morning, they headed north to Fairbanks to replenish the supplies which had dwindled, making sure to get enough for the two of them. Gwen's experience with stocking a cafe helped, though at first Denny thought she was overstocking. It turned out she knew what she was doing.

After their shopping was done, Denny called up Nathan Barker. Surprisingly, he was home. Denny drove up to the house so Gwen and Nathan could meet each other.

When Nathan opened the door and saw the two of them standing there, he was obviously very glad to see them. They got comfortably settled with some hot brandy to chase the chill away, talking happily together.

Nathan was home working on plans for a large new office building to be built in Fairbanks. The renderings of the building showed a very nicely designed structure, and the most interesting thing was that it was a single story, very efficiently set up to keep maintenance costs down.

Barker insisted they have dinner with him and stay the night. The two homesteaders were happy to do so. Gwen could see that Denny and Nathan had a strong bond between them. Caraway had told Gwen about Caroline's plane crash and the aftermath, but Gwen could see that the two men's connection went beyond that. When Denny suggested that Nathan show Gwen his game room, he was hesitant, not knowing Gwen as Denny did, but she was delighted to see all Nathan's trophies and impressed him with her general knowledge of game animals, even from Africa and Asia. She told Barker that at one time she had planned on going to school to be a wildlife biologist. Denny told her he didn't know that.

"Well, Mr. Caraway, there is a lot you don't know, yet."

"I hope not," he said, "I'm having trouble keeping up with you already."

The three of them had a chuckle over that.

Barker had a good breakfast cooking when the two got up the next morning. "Can't go out in the bush without a good meal in your bellies, yes?"

Gwen and Denny nodded their agreement, and started in on the big meal, which included fresh fruit and rolls.

Before they left, Caroline walked in the front door. There was a moment between her and Denny which Gwen didn't miss.

The two of them chatted a few minutes before he and Gwen said their good-byes. Driving away, Gwen was silent, and Denny knew exactly why.

"Gwen?"

"Denny."

"Is there anything you want to ask me?"

"Is there anything I need to know, Mr. Caraway?"

"Absolutely nothing."

"Then no, I'm fine."

Denny had gotten Gwen a good ski mask. He'd noticed a couple of spots on her face, signs of frostbite, and didn't want it to get worse. On the trail ride back home, the snow began coming down heavily, and soon turned into whiteout conditions. They stopped about half-way home and considered whether to return to Salcha to wait out the weather or continue on. Gwen refused to turn around, so Denny told her to stick close and keep an eye on his snow machine's taillight.

He held his speed down to make it easier for her, though he knew she could keep up at higher speeds. The whiteout was in full strength, but Caraway had taken the winter trail so many times he was able to run it almost by instinct, thinking about the next stretch ahead, and they made it home safe and sound.

When they pulled up in the front yard, Denny walked over and asked Gwen if it had been okay for her.

"It was no problem, Mr. Caraway. Maybe next time though, you'll remember the sled blocks the taillight from view."

Denny knew Gwen wasn't seriously scolding him, but he was embarrassed about it anyway.

Before the end of winter, Denny got to experience Gwen's abilities to survive in the bush. The moose meat hadn't lasted as long as expected. They had taken Elliot a nice load of meat when they had gone out to get supplies, and now they had to restock the cache. Since winter was winding down, a whole moose would leave a lot of meat to thaw in the spring, but they had a hand meat grinder, a pressure cooker, and plenty of quart jars, so processing the rest of the meat would be no problem.

It was nearly March, and the weather had risen to fifteen above, though it could plummet into the sub zeros at any time. Denny and Gwen got all geared up and went looking for a nice barren cow or small bull, both better eating than an old bull.

They hiked about a mile along their side of Lanyard Creek before they saw some fairly fresh moose tracks. It seemed to be a group of three animals. They hadn't gone several hundred yards more, moving as quietly as possible on their snowshoes, when they saw the three moose ahead of them in the open, just outside the edge of thick forest. There were two cows and a young bull, perhaps two to three years old.

Moving closer to Denny, Gwen whispered in a soft voice, "The young bull looks good."

Denny nodded. Without another word, Gwen dropped her snowshoes, and slipped into the trees, quickly moving out of sight. Denny wondered what she was up to. When he looked back at the moose, barely fifty yards away, they were looking right at him, and a moment later they broke for the trees.

Denny suddenly realized what Gwen had planned to do, and moved out into the clearing, over to where the moose had been, and waited. Perhaps five minutes later, he heard a loud BOOM! coming from the trees. He broke into a fast trot, following the moose tracks into the trees. Denny was brought up quickly by the sight of the two cow moose standing close on his right, their hackles up, ears laid back, staring at something he couldn't quite see, though he knew what he'd find.

Sure enough, after a short walk into the trees, avoiding the angry cow moose, he found Gwen, her pack off, knives out, trying to work the moose into position to start field dressing, and that was a lot of weight to move around.

Looking up at Denny, she smiled and said, "About time you got here. Give me a hand with this big boy." Denny gave a single silent chuckle and went to work with his able partner.

He saw she had made a perfect heart shot and the big bullet had, according to Gwen, knocked the moose down like a bolt of lightning. She talked while they worked, and Denny listened. "Dad made sure I learned to make the first shot count. He started me off on rabbits and spruce hens with an old twenty-two. The first time he let me shoot his big gun, I was fourteen and a skinny kid, no remarks please. It actually knocked me half over. My dad was ready. He stood behind me and kept me from hitting the ground. My shoulder hurt for days. I got good with it though, and brought home meat a few times after Dad died.

"For all she had done, Momma wasn't a hunter. Couldn't bring herself to shoot a moose or even a black bear, though she did shoot one that had gotten into the cafe's kitchen when they first opened the place. When I asked her why she could shoot the bear in the kitchen, she said it was because he was 'being rude.' Momma could shoot, even though she didn't do it much."

A little over an hour later, they had the young bull dressed and quartered. Denny and Gwen decided they could get the snow machine and big sled close enough to minimize the work needed to haul all that meat home. Gwen volunteered to go get the snow machine and sled, and Denny okayed her without hesitation.

Denny realized he had a real treasure. He wondered what else he would find out about Gwen before all was said and done. He figured they had plenty of time to learn each other, yet, he suspected she'd come to fully know him well before he learned everything about her.

Twenty minutes later, he heard Gwen bringing the rig out onto the little meadow outside the trees. It was a short easy distance for them to load all the meat in the big sled and haul it back to the cabin. They spent the next few hours butchering up the moose, putting it in game bags, and stashing it in the cache. They were going to hang the meat on the cross pole tied on between two small spruce, but they had seen some wolf tracks on their hike out and didn't want to take any chances. They probably had six weeks and maybe a little more before they would have to process and can the meat. Until then, they were well stocked with fresh cuts. After they had washed up, Denny swept Gwen into his arms and said, "You did well out there, my love, I'm proud of you."

Gwen pulled back a little, and went into a funny little routine, hanging her head, putting her hands behind her back and acting the shy girl, rubbing one foot on the floor. "Aw, shucks, Mr. Denny, it weren't nuthin'!"

Gwen was amazed when Denny broke out in real laughter. She'd never heard him laugh like that before. Likewise, Denny had never seen Gwen being silly before.

As was bound to happen, Gwen did some rearranging of the cabin's interior. Denny wasn't sure what to expect, but what he had already discovered about Gwen told him to simply let her do whatever she felt needed doing.

Gwen basically moved things around so her own possessions blended right in with what Denny already had in the cabin. It was amazing to him that when she was finished, it looked pretty much the same, only with more inside including the several pieces of furniture she had brought, small items she didn't want to leave behind. When she was finished, all the new furnishings looked as though they belonged there.

Denny told Gwen he had a lot of milled boards in the old cabin to be used for shelves or cabinets. Her eyes lit up at that. So, during the last real month of winter, Denny made several open-front cabinets and added three nice shelves to the cabin. Though Gwen wasn't a frilly sort of woman, she had some nice things to go on shelves — *chachkas*, she called them, for the sake of dressing up the place. She had managed to bring in the crystal whiskey glasses and several goblets without breakage.

Denny found no fault with anything Gwen did, though if he had, she never would have known.

Chapter Twenty Three

Spring came in quickly. The temperature rose steadily and break-up lasted only a few weeks, despite heavy snowfall that winter. There were a number of days when a warm wind blew down the Salcha River corridor, melting the snow at a rapid pace. For a while, Gwen and Denny were worried about flooding. The Salcha rose high and fast, and so Lanyard Creek followed suit. The new cabin was back far enough to be safe from high water. The flood waters reached the pilings of the old cabin. Fortunately, it did no real damage. Still, it was a little worrisome until the water began to recede.

One morning Denny came out to see how conditions were, and while scanning the creek saw something unexpected and disturbing. Caught in a mass of branches and other water-carried debris, a hand and forearm was sticking up out of the tangle. He walked as close as he could get and saw it was a man who had somehow drowned, probably in the Salcha, and been washed into Lanyard. Denny got a length of rope from the old cabin, tied one end to one of the foundation posts, the other around his waist. He waded out in the strong current the short distance to where the body was caught up and tried to remove it. Caraway found that he needed to cut away some of the branches. Wading back to the bank, he got his Swede saw, went back out, and cut away what was holding the body prisoner. Struggling against the creek, which seemed to want to keep its macabre possession, Denny managed to pull the man up to the bank. Gwen was now outside watching, a dark look on her face.

Gently laying the body down, Caraway went inside the cabin to get into some dry clothes. Gwen insisted he sit and have a cup of hot tea until the shivering brought on by being in the icy water subsided.

"Do you know him, Denny?"

"No, never saw him before. He could have been carried a long way, maybe even from the campsites near the highway. He looks Native. Whatever the details, I have to take him in, and soon."

Gwen would have been fine staying alone on the homestead under normal circumstances. This situation, however, put her in a different frame of mind. Looking at Denny with a slight pleading in her eyes, she said, "Fine, I'm going with you." Seeing the look in her eyes, he simply nodded.

They carried the body into the old cabin away from any roaming predators. Early the next morning, wrapping him in a blanket tied to stay in place, they put him in the plastic ATV trailer Denny had purchased the year before.

The trail was in pretty good shape for the ride, though quite boggy in some spots. The bridge Denny built had been damaged slightly by the high, fast-running water, but it was still solid enough to let them cross safely.

Gwen sat behind Denny, and though she was a tough Alaska woman, she wearied of hearing the poor soul bumping and bouncing along behind her in the little trailer. Knowing what was making the sounds began to weigh on her mind. Finally, she asked Denny to go a little slower. He wondered if the ride was banging her around too much, and she told him, "It's not me I'm thinking about." Denny caught on right away and he slowed down a bit. Still, they got to the highway before six p.m., so the North Star Cafe was still open.

Charlie Brady was starting to close down when Denny and Gwen walked in. From the looks on their faces he knew something was up. Denny took him out to the wheeler while Gwen sat quietly inside. She was glad the journey with their unfortunate cargo was over.

Charlie and Denny carried the man over to a small refrigerated outbuilding next to the cafe used to store perishable foods, and laid him on the floor before Brady called the troopers to come out. As it happened, there was an officer about an hour away. The three of them sat quietly waiting for him to arrive, making small talk, though little conversation actually passed between them.

About forty minutes later, a Alaska State Trooper in an SUV pulled up and came in. Charlie didn't know the young man, though the officer knew Brady by reputation.

He inspected the body, found the victim's wallet in a buttoned shirt pocket, located his ID, asked Denny some pertinent questions, and took some photographs. They loaded the man up in the SUV. Charlie talked to the young trooper for a few minutes, shook his hand, and then the officer drove away north.

It was a relief to have the situation concluded. Charlie told them the drowned man had been missing for two days, having fallen into the Salcha when the bank gave way beneath him. The swift current and debris-filled water had done the rest.

"The trooper confided in me there was drinking going on, no big surprise. The man was from Fairbanks. He and his family were on a spring road trip, headed down to the Kenai, and had stopped at the campsite to stay for a couple of days. Apparently he fell in their first evening there."

"Sad for the family," was all Gwen said. They bid Charlie goodnight and headed over to the trailer for some sleep. As they were settling in, Gwen asked,

"Denny, would you consider taking a little trip for a day or two? I'd like to put a little time between this incident and going back home."

"I think that's a good idea, Gwen. What say we drive down to Anchorage, to roam around a bit and motel it?"

"You bet. Think we could go to a store to buy some fabric? I'd like to make curtains for the cabin windows."

"Sure Gwen, and we could pick up some extra bulk food while we're at it."

"I hope all this domestication isn't too rough on you, Mr. Caraway."

"Not a bit, and if it gets too pleasant, I'll go find a bear to annoy, to put things right."

"Well, don't expect me to repair your torn-up clothes if you do."

Their plans settled, they kissed and curled up together for some much needed rest.

Traveling to Anchorage proved to be a good thing. It took them away from the unfortunate situation of the drowned man and provided a break from their daily routine, even though they loved it. Once in the city, Gwen got to browse through several stores' fabric sections, finding some nice blue corduroy for the curtains in one. At first she teased Denny, pretending to want some really gaudy flowered cotton, over the top even for a Hawaiian shirt. Denny took it in stride, willing to accept anything she wanted to use. He was relieved though, when she settled on the solid blue material. He never knew she had been teasing him, and she never told him.

The two of them spent a night in a motel. Though it wasn't a special thing for Denny, who would have preferred to stay in his cabin, Gwen enjoyed it thoroughly, especially the long hot bath she took. While she bathed, he went out and picked up some take-out Chinese food, another treat rarely had by the homesteader. The next day, they had breakfast at Gwennie's, where he had eaten with Nathan Barker on their trip to Anchorage. It was considered an authentic

Alaska restaurant. For Denny, it didn't seem that special, though he liked the reindeer sausage, and planned on making some the next time he took a caribou. He told Gwen she should have a stake in the restaurant, considering the name, and she replied she had no desire to ever have anything to do with a restaurant again. "Besides, Mr. Caraway, you know how I feel about being called Gwennie." Denny flashed a quick grin, remembering full well the only time, years ago, he had called her Gwennie, and the negative reaction he had gotten.

After picking up a few staples, they gassed up the truck and headed north. Despite the brief time they were there, the two of them were happy to leave the city and head back home. The drive north was uneventful but pleasant, their conversation making the miles roll by more quickly.

It was good getting back to the homestead. Even Gwen was glad to be alone again, just the two of them. She was adapting to the isolated life, having been surrounded by more than her share of people after years at the cafe, and with her large circle of friends, though it had diminished over the years.

Gwen had already been experiencing the same type of changes Denny went through when he had begun homesteading, the "clearing" of his senses, being away from all the noise, excessive lights, and smells of urban living. Her sight and sense of smell had sharpened, and she was able to see things differently, without the excessive input she had experienced, even in a little town such as Hazel.

One day, she questioned Denny while they were sitting comfortably in the cabin together, about something that concerned her.

"Denny, do you ever seem to hear voices while you're out somewhere? Sometimes I think I do, and wonder if I'm losing it, being out here in the bush all the time."

Denny chuckled and told Gwen, "Yeah, I had some funny moments after I'd been on my first homestead for a while, and yes, I do hear faint voices, especially if there's a bit of a breeze blowing. I never have resolved it, and the few people I've asked about it, such as Ed Gundross, who had heard them too, didn't know for sure what it was. Truth to tell, I think it has something to do with the land itself. The bush is alive, so who's to say if somehow we don't tap into what's going on, being a regular part of things out here."

That gave Gwen food for thought. Though she wasn't the spiritual person Denny was, or had become, she valued his perception of things, and let it go, after telling Denny she wished she could understand what the voices were saying.

Still, even after their discussion, when she heard the voices they gave her a little case of the willies.

Chapter Twenty Four

A few weeks after they had taken the body into Salcha, Denny and Gwen had unexpected visitors. Of course, any visitors to their remote location were unusual. They were in the cabin having some soup in the middle of the day when they heard the sounds of wheelers coming in.

Going outside, they saw Charlie Brady on an ATV, with an old Native woman sitting behind him, and another wheeler with two younger people on it. It was extremely rare for him to come out to the homestead, usually on some official business when he was still on duty. Denny sensed this was because of the man they had found.

The old woman hopped off the wheeler before Brady had dismounted. Her spryness belied her visible age.

With a sparkle in her eye she said, "That mister Brady must have hit every bad bump he could find, just to beat up my old bones!"

Charlie smiled at Denny and winked. "Denny, I've brought you some special guests. This sweet old girl is Emma Pete, the mother of the man you found. The other two folks here are Dorothy and Robert, his children. His wife couldn't come out. They wanted to meet and thank you for what you did, so I guided them out today. You've done some good trail work. The ride was a lot easier than I expected, and you built a good bridge."

Emma came up to Denny and took both his hands. Her action caught him off guard, so he just stood there, waiting for her to speak. Emma gave him a long look with her clear, bright eyes, but said nothing. It became obvious to him how grateful she was, even without her speaking. Then she went over to Gwen and did the same. Gwen couldn't help herself, and gave Emma a long hug.

Taking a step back, Emma said, "You two people were very kind to do what you did for a stranger. We all want to thank you so much for bringing Henry home to us. We weren't sure if we'd ever see him again. That devil alcohol finally took him from us. We tried to help him, but it's a hard path to walk away from."

Then Dorothy and Robert came over and shook hands with them both. Gwen and Denny invited them in to have something to eat, and they all went inside the cabin. Emma and Dorothy sat at the little table, while Denny, Charlie, and Robert stood with coffee mugs in hand, and Gwen got busy preparing a meal. The elderly woman and her granddaughter got up and went over to chat with her and to help.

"My dad was a hard man," Robert told the other men. "He could be mean when he drank, but he always took care of us and was a good hunter even when he was into his bottle. We will miss him. At least we have him nearby now, instead of being lost somewhere, thanks to you." Out of his jacket pocket, he took an old hunting knife in a stained leather sheath, with a well-worn blade obviously sharpened many times, and offered it to Denny. "I would like you to have this; it was my dad's."

That got to Denny. He thanked Robert and patted him on the shoulder, while Charlie looked on and nodded knowingly.

The little group of people spent time together in the log cabin, talking about Henry and village life, and what it was like for them to live in Fairbanks. Gwen made salmon chowder from fish they had caught in Lanyard Creek and canned up, and some fry bread, using Denny's recipe. They all stood or sat, quietly talking and having the meal together. Emma remarked the fry bread was good, just like they made at home. Denny told her where and how he got the recipe. The old woman smiled and nodded approvingly at the story.

Dorothy took out some smoked salmon from a carry bag she had brought. It was the best Denny, Gwen, and Charlie had ever tried. Emma smiled and said the flavor came from an old Athabascan recipe. When Gwen asked her what it was, Emma smiled widely and said, "It's marinated in Kikkoman Soy Sauce." And then she laughed a laugh that filled the cabin, and soon they were all laughing with her.

When the hour grew late, the Petes put up a tent in the yard beside the cabin to spend the night. It was a long ride back to the road, and Emma especially needed to rest.

Charlie, Denny, and Robert stayed up a while, standing by the creek, talking about life in general, or simply standing, sharing the moment. Though the three of them had different stories to tell, they shared a common bond, the Alaska bush, and didn't need to talk to appreciate each other's company.

Dorothy yelled from the tent flap, "Robert, Emma says to come get some sleep!" Robert grinned and said, "I better go, or Emma won't give me any peace. See you in the morning."

Denny helped Charlie put up his small tent. It was stained and patched in several places, Charlie having used it for years, while working and hunting.

Gwen got up early, having set a large bowl of sourdough starter overnight to make flapjacks in the morning, and brewed a full pot of coffee. When everyone was up, they had a fine breakfast of pancakes, eggs, and lots of coffee, as well as more smoked salmon. The little group sat a while afterwards, quietly visiting. They all knew that it was unlikely they would come together again, but there was a bond between them now that would always be there.

All too soon, it was time for the Petes and Charlie to head back to Salcha. Dorothy gave Gwen a beautiful beaded hair clasp, and then they all said good-bye. Denny told them they could come visit any time and if they ever needed anything, to let him know.

"You already gave us the best thing possible, Denny Caraway," Emma said. "You are a good man."

Charlie said he'd see them soon, and then they left, the wheelers grumbling off into the distance.

Denny and Gwen stood listening until all sounds of the departure faded away, leaving them once again to their home by the creek. Although the two of them agreed it had been a special time, they were still glad to get back to their regular routines. Gwen went inside to straighten up and Denny began stockpiling more firewood, a never-ending task in the bush.

Chapter Twenty Five

When Denny wasn't gathering wood for the next winter and working on a bath house, he and Gwen took hikes so she could get familiar with the country. Later that summer, she and Denny caught silver salmon as they made their run up Lanyard. They smoked much of the fish and canned a large amount too. It was a good supplement to the left-over moose meat they had canned up in early spring. They went to a large meadow about two miles from the homestead where Denny picked berries, and Gwen went crazy, picking all she could load into the several tin cans they'd brought along. There were blueberries, crowberries, and even some low bush cranberries in the middle of the meadow. Both the cans were full in no time. Gwen wanted to go back while the berries were still going strong, and several days later she and Denny returned. As they began hiking back to the cabin, he stopped and turned to look at the meadow. Denny quietly told Gwen to look, and she saw that a big bear had come out of the trees at the far edge of the meadow and begun browsing.

"When I last came out here, Gwen, in the middle of picking I looked up to see a big grizzly grazing on berries not one hundred yards from me. Well, even though I would normally move away to put some space between us, it felt okay the way it was, so I kept on picking and kept one eye on the old bruiser. By the time my bucket was full, he had closed the gap by half, but seemed perfectly content to share the berries with me. Still, you never know about bears, so I slowly drifted away and headed back to the cabin."

"Do you think this is the same bear?"

"I don't know, Gwen. Let's head home."

The next morning, Denny woke up to find Gwen gone, a fresh pot of coffee cooking on the stove. A note on the table said: "Denny, I just had to get some more berries. Don't worry, I have Dad's rifle with me. You get back on the firewood, mister.

Love, Gwen."

At first, Denny was concerned, and was going to head out to the meadow, then he stopped himself, realizing it was better to let her be. She was Alaskan born and bred, and would be all right. Besides, she probably wouldn't appreciate him trailing her, as if he didn't think she could handle some berry picking. Denny made himself a big peanut butter and honey sandwich on some sourdough bread, swilled down a mug of coffee, and went out to cut and split more firewood.

In mid-afternoon, Gwen came back with both buckets full. Denny had worked up a big stack of split firewood and knocked off for the day to help Gwen with her treasure.

"Were you worried about me, Mister Caraway?"

"Why would I be worried Gwen, you can handle yourself out there. I got busy on the firewood as I was ordered to by my boss lady."

"Oh, poo, just help me with these berries."

In the evening, they canned most of the berries for later use. Gwen left some out and made a delicious berry upside down cake that they ate late that night, sitting quietly at the table, enjoying the evening and one another's company.

"I love you."

"What did you just say, Denny?"

"I love you. Want to tie the knot and make things legal?"

Gwen grew quiet, thinking, giving Denny a serious look as she did. Caraway held his tongue, waiting for her to answer.

"Is that something you need, Denny?"

"Actually Gwen, I'm fine the way things are. I thought you might want to get hitched."

"No, I'm good, but if you feel the same way a year from now, let's do it, okay?"

"Works for me."

When they went to bed, Denny noticed Gwen was somehow sweeter and more open when they made love. His offer must have touched her, he decided. Next year, he would remember to ask again.

The days and weeks went by, full of shared moments for the two homesteaders. Whether it was daily chores, or exciting times in the bush, it all went to making their life together better than either could have expected or hoped for. Gwen knew living with Denny on his remote homestead was going to be wonderful, and she was never disappointed. She knew it was good for Denny too. She could tell by his behavior, the smiles and laughter coming from him. The seriousness which had dominated his demeanor had faded, though when something needed to be done, he was all business.

The incident that made Gwen realize how much Denny was a part of the country, happened one late summer morning when they had walked out of the cabin together to go down to the creek for water. Rounding the corner, they had come face to face with a mother grizzly and her two cubs walking along the bank. Immediately the mother bear went into defensive mode and Gwen was positive they were in for a bad time.

Denny, seemingly unshaken by the situation, began talking calmly and quietly to the bear, who was moving her front end side to side, not sure what she was going to do, moaning in distress. Gwen was wise enough to stand still and listen to Denny.

"Hey, mama, it's okay, we're not going to hurt your kids. They're really nice cubs and I hope they have a good long life. We'll wait until you're gone before we get our water. There's no trouble here, no trouble."

When he first began talking, the bear took a couple of steps forward, and Gwen thought a charge was coming, but the bear stopped moving and seemed to be listening to Denny. Finally, she slowly turned away, keeping an eye on the two humans. The cubs had already run away some distance up the creek, and the mother bear soon joined them, and they continued on their way.

Gwen didn't relax until the bears were out of sight, and Denny didn't move, either.

Gwen said, "I think I need a cup of coffee."

"Sounds like a good idea to me, Gwen, a very good idea."

Chapter Twenty Six

Two years went by, good years and full. Life, however, has a way of putting people on a different path, when least expected or desired.

Denny walked out of the cabin to find Gwen sitting on the wood splitting stump, her arms on her legs, head hanging down.

"Gwen, are you okay?"

"I don't know, Denny, I was splitting some wood and I got dizzy, and now I have some pain in my abdomen. Think I'll lie down a while." Gwen got up slowly and went into the cabin, Denny following right behind her, quite concerned.

"Don't worry, Mr. Caraway, I'll be fine, just need a rest. Probably woman stuff. At my age, things change."

Still, Denny was worried of course. He kept looking in on her as he went about his daily chores. Gwen slept for hours, and he finally came in and made some meat broth for her to have when she woke up. When she did wake up and drank some of the broth from a mug, she went outside and got sick, finally coming back in to lie down again.

The next morning, she seemed okay, though she only had a piece of toasted sourdough bread and some tea. Gwen went out to the old cabin to get a hoe to clear between the rows of vegetables they had started indoors and transplanted when the soil warmed up. She had only worked a short while when she leaned the hoe against the cabin wall and went inside to sit in her chair.

When Denny came in from hauling several ten-foot lengths of wood behind the wheeler for cutting and splitting, he saw through the open door Gwen sleeping in the chair. Now he was really upset. This wasn't like her at all.

As the days went on, she continued to have no appetite and began losing weight, continued to be tired, and complained of pain in her gut. She stubbornly refused to go out with Denny to Fairbanks to get a check-up, until the pain got so bad one day she collapsed, doubled up on the floor.

The next morning, Denny put Gwen up behind him on the wheeler, and they headed to the road. It took longer than usual because he rode very slowly. When they got to the highway, Denny rode right over to the North Star Cafe.

Gwen remained sitting on the wheeler when he went in to see Charlie Brady. When he told him what was happening, Charlie told him to get her right up to Fairbanks memorial. "I'm not going to say what I think Denny. I am familiar with these symptoms, because my wife had them. Just get her up there. I'm going to call the doctor who took care of my wife, and let him know you're coming. He's very capable, and someone you can trust."

Troubled by Charlie's words, Denny took Gwen over to the trailer, got the truck running, and headed up the highway, going as fast as was safe, and sometimes faster.

A life which had been ideal had turned into something dark and disturbing. Denny had never been in a situation such as this. He had never cared for someone as he did for Gwen. She had become the center of his world.

She sat silently on the seat, head back with her eyes closed, wincing once and a while. Denny felt impotent. He had always been able to take care of things, and this situation was something he had no control over and he didn't like it.

When they got up to the hospital, he took her into the E.R. and asked for Dr. Hanover, who came down in a few minutes, introduced himself, and began giving orders to the nurses about how to deal with Gwen.

"I'm sorry Denny, but you'll need to wait until I figure out what is going on. It could be a while. I talked to Charlie Brady on the phone and he told me what you had said. He's a good man. If you're a friend of his, I'm glad to help." Walking away, he left Denny to wait and worry.

It was some hours later when Dr. Hanover showed up again.

"Mr. Caraway, we've run some initial tests and I'm sorry to tell you this, but it is quite likely your wife has cancer, probably pancreatic. We'll have to do some exploratory surgery to be sure."

Denny stood there in disbelief. This wasn't supposed to be, not for her, not for them.

"Doc, you do what you have to do to be sure. I have to tell you, we don't have medical coverage. We're homesteaders. We have some money but I don't know if. . ."

"Denny, don't worry about the money for now. Let's just see what we find. I can schedule her for tomorrow morning. I don't have anything else this important going on right now, so we'll just get her in, okay?"

Denny just nodded slightly.

"We have her sedated on pain medication, but you can see her if you like. She probably won't be very communicative."

Of course, Denny did. Gwen was very groggy, drugged up as she was, but she knew he was there and held onto his hand, until she was sleeping quietly.

Caraway felt things were way over his head as he walked out of the hospital later into the fresh air. The nurse had told him to come back in the morning if he liked, because Gwen would definitely be sleeping through the night.

Denny didn't know what to do. Finally he started up the truck and went to see the only person he knew in Fairbanks, Nathan Barker.

When he drove up to Chena Ridge and knocked on the door of the beautiful log house, he didn't notice its wonderful construction. The door opened and a petite blonde woman opened the door. She was Nathan's ex, Caroline's mother, someone he had met once before at the house. She took one look at Denny's face and called out to Nathan. She explained to Denny, "He's just back from Taiwan. There's a big project he's putting together there. Oh, here he is now."

Nathan was smiling when he came up to shake Caraway's hand, but seeing the look on Denny's face, the smile disappeared.

"Denny, you look like you could use a drink."

"It would be good if that was all I needed, Nathan."

They settled in Barker's den, with two glasses of bourbon, and Denny told Nathan why he was in Fairbanks. The obvious concern on his friend's face made Denny feel self-conscious, and he said as much. Nathan told him it was fine he had come, and anything he could do, he would. He offered Denny a place to stay while he was in town.

Nathan was another solid, decent man, as was Ed Gundross, Charlie Brady, and George Whiting too, the old fellow he had bought his first homestead land from. He felt fortunate to know these men, two of them gone now.

After a while, Nathan suggested they get some rest. He had returned from the Orient a few hours before and was very tired. He told Denny the room he had stayed in before was all made up, and he should consider it home until he had to do something else. Denny gave the man a warm handshake and went to get some sleep, which didn't come until the early morning hours.

Denny showered up and went over to the hospital. Gwen was just going into surgery when he got there. He had a moment to hold her hand and kiss her forehead before she was wheeled into the O.R.

He sat in the waiting room, barely controlling his emotions. Denny hated waiting for anything, and it was all he could do to sit still, imagining what was going on. He finally went out to his truck, broke out his pipe and tobacco, and had a smoke. Normally, this would have calmed him down, but not this time. Tapping out the half-burned tobacco, he went back inside to sit again.

It was another two hours before Dr. Hanover came in. He had his paper mask down around his neck and Denny couldn't help but notice the several tiny blood stains on his scrubs. He gave an involuntary little jerk of his head.

"Sit down, Denny, let's talk."

"Just tell me what's going on Doc, please."

Knowing this man wanted straight talk, Hanover responded, "Gwen has advanced pancreatic cancer. It's been spreading for some time. It's often hard to catch right away. We could operate, but it is so metastasized I'm afraid we would only cause her more discomfort without resolving the problem. The pancreas and liver are completely involved. I'm sorry."

"Would chemotherapy help?"

"I'm sorry, Mr. Caraway, it has gone too far, and is too intrusive. I think chemo would only cause her great discomfort, and probably weaken her further."

"Well, what the hell can we do?"

"I hate having to tell you this, but the best thing to do is to make her as comfortable as possible, and not much more. You're entitled to another opinion of course. You can see her in a couple of hours, but we'll probably keep her on some pain meds. If there is anything I can do, let me know."

The doctor began walking away, and then turned and said, "Oh, a Nathan Barker called the hospital. He said, since you are an employee of his, you're fully covered. He gave all your pertinent information. I'll see you tomorrow."

Denny stood there in the impersonal waiting room, numb from what the doctor had told him. When his mind cleared, he went to see Gwen, who was still asleep. He sat next to her bed, surrounded by monitors and plastic lines, trying to make sense of it. He couldn't. Denny fell asleep in the chair.

"Denny," a faint voice called. Again, "Denny." He woke up to see Gwen looking at him through dulled eyes. Reaching over, he took her hand. She squeezed his slightly.

Chapter Twenty Six

"Did you talk to the doctor?"

"Yes, my love, I did."

"They're not going to be able to fix me, are they?"

Denny sat looking at his sweetheart, before shaking his head. A tear rolled out of his eye.

"Don't you dare, Denny Caraway, don't you dare." You stay strong, Mr. Homesteader, please."

Denny found the strength to get himself together, for Gwen.

Dr. Hanover came in just then, to talk to Gwen. "Has Denny talked to you about things?"

"He didn't have to, doctor. I know what's happening. How long do I have to stay here?"

"A couple of days. Do you plan on returning to your homestead? Is it a rough ride?"

Denny nodded. "Pretty rough; we'd have to take an ATV in. But we have a trailer in Salcha we can stay in a while, until her incisions have healed."

"How long do we have?" Gwen asked.

Denny looked down when she asked the doctor.

"Not long, I'm afraid, Gwen; weeks, perhaps a few months. But the last bit of time will be pretty hard without pain meds, which we will provide for you."

"No more pain medicine," Gwen said as firmly as she could. Looking at Denny, she said, with a pleading look. "There are two things I want from you, Mr. Caraway."

"Just name it, Gwen."

"I want you to marry me, and I want to go home, soon."

Denny looked at the doctor.

Hanover said, "We have a chaplain here at the hospital. Shall I get him?"

Before Denny could reply, Gwen said to the doctor, "Yeah, go get him, I'll wait here," and winked at him.

After the doctor left, Gwen asked Denny if he thought they were rushing into things. That got a little smile from him.

"Denny, we have to find a way to get me home soon. I can feel it."

"I'll find a way, I promise."

Just then, the doctor returned with a man carrying a bible and some papers. A few minutes later, Gwen and Denny were married, using two little rubber bands for rings. It was a bittersweet moment for Denny, but it brought Gwen some joy, so he was glad.

Gwen needed to rest then, so after thanking the chaplain and the doctor and nurse who were witnesses to the marriage, Denny left her side, and went over to the Barker house. Nathan was distraught by what Denny told him, and restated his willingness to help with whatever Denny needed. Denny said he needed to take him up on the offer and told him of his plan. Nathan said, "That's no problem, Denny, no problem at all. Just tell me when. I'll be here another week, getting some final details in order for the Taiwan project. It's big, the most complex piece of work we've ever done. But, let's make things work for you and your dear wife first."

The next day, Denny talked to Dr. Hanover, discussing what he should expect and what he would need. They spent the rest of the day getting things arranged.

Two mornings later they had Gwen ready, and at noon a helicopter belonging to Barker Surveying landed at the hospital heliport to take Gwen and Denny to the homestead. A short time later they were there, Gwen handling the flight well, the amazing views from the helicopter helping to take her mind off her condition.

Nathan Barker went with them and helped Denny get Gwen all settled in, with the supplies the hospital gave them. Five minutes later, they were alone again in their cabin. Being back seemed to make Gwen feel better.

Denny took stock of what he had brought for her. He read the detailed instructions, planning to follow them exactly, and had everything neatly arranged on the little spruce table.

The next morning, Denny heard the sound of a chopper coming in, and went outside to see his wheeler suspended under the Barker helicopter. They gently set it down and hovered while Denny unhooked the cargo straps, waved, and watched the chopper go. A note taped to the top of the seat said, "Denny, anything, any time. God Bless, Nathan." A lump formed in Caraway's throat. Going inside, he shut the door to see to his wife's needs.

The next six weeks were filled with moments of tears, joy, and pain. Loyal and devoted to her as he was, Denny took care of Gwen in all the ways she needed. The hardest thing was when Gwen could no longer eat, except for water and tea. He had brought out some cottage cheese and yogurt, keeping it in the cooler box. After a while, even that was too much. His tough Alaska wife quickly withered away in front of him. The two sweethearts spent hours talking about their lives, the high and low points, their dreams and desires.

It got to the point that Gwen was sleeping more than she was awake. She had become sensitive to any physical contact, because of the pain, and had begun asking for pain medication. Denny couldn't sleep close to her and either slept on a pallet of blankets and sleeping bags on the floor, or sat up for hours, dozing off in Gwen's old family chair, which he put right next to the bed.

And then, one morning, he awoke to Gwen's hand on his arm, but she was gone, a little smile on her face. He remembered her saying in a tiny voice the night before, "As long as I'm with you now, it's okay."

He had replied, hardly able to speak, "You'll always be with me, Gwen."

Denny sat there for hours, not making a sound, holding Gwen's hand.

He walked up the rise between the cabin and the little lake, and dug her grave between two young birches. The soil was full of cobbles, but Denny kept going until it was done to his satisfaction.

Going to the cabin, he wrapped Gwen in her favorite quilt, made by her maternal grandmother in Ireland, carried her up the low hill, and gently placed her in the ground. Though not a very religious man, he said a silent prayer when she was covered, asking God to take her to him and keep her safe. Unable to hold it in, he said out loud, "You blessed me when you brought her into my life and cursed me when you took her away." The toughened home-steader fell to his knees then, and cried as only the truly broken-hearted can.

Denny had left no marker, so he alone knew where Gwen lay. It was the way she wanted it.

For the next two days, Denny sat in the cabin, not eating or drinking, merely sitting as if in a trance. If a bear or wolf had wandered in, it wouldn't have made any difference.

Then, on the morning of the third day, as if he had gone through some metamorphosis, Denny got up, drank several dippers full of water, and made himself a good breakfast.

Taking only his .44, and his Winchester 30-06, Denny headed the wheeler down the trail towards the road. There were things he had to do.

Denny let caution go by the wayside as he rode the wheeler fast and hard. He reached the road sooner than ever before. Riding over to the North Star Cafe, he took the Winchester in with him. Charlie Brady looked up in surprise to see him walking in, rifle in hand.

Walking up to Charlie, he handed him the rifle, and said, simply, "Take care of this for me Charlie."

Taken off-guard, Brady was going to say something, until he saw what was in Denny's eyes, the pain and intense sadness, and something else he didn't like. There was a powerful glint of anger there, too. Charlie realized there was only one thing that would have allowed Denny to come in alone. Gwen was gone. As soon as the realization came to Brady, Denny, who must have seen it, nodded, turned and left.

Denny went over to the trailer, found the title and went to Eliot's home. Elliot's grandson was working in the yard. When Elliot saw Denny at the door and let him in, he knew almost immediately what was up. There was no way Denny would be there alone unless he truly was by himself. Denny kept talk to a minimum, telling Elliot he was giving him the trailer and he could let his grandson stay there if he wanted. Elliot, being the wise old fellow, simply nodded, shook Denny's hand, and watched the woodsman go out to his wheeler and disappear.

Caraway rode back in on the trail to the homestead as fast as he had ridden out. Going into the old cabin, he ate some moose jerky and fry bread, took his big pack from the old cabin, and began putting basic necessities into it, until he had everything he figured he needed. Looking around, he nodded to himself, walked out of the cabin without closing the door, and strapped the pack onto the wheeler's rear rack. Slipping Gwen's father's rifle over his head and shoulder by the sling, he started up the wheeler and headed down the back trail behind the cabin, going deeper into the bush. When he ran out of any trail, he bushwhacked until the ATV ran out of gas, dismounted, hoisted the pack and walked away.

Chapter Twenty Seven

Summer was winding down. The first frost hadn't appeared in the morning hours yet, and the leaves on the birches and aspens had only begun turning. There were still a few days of August left.

Charlie Brady had hoped there might be a little resurgence of the warmer part of summer, but it hadn't come. The thermometer read thirty-six degrees when he opened the cafe that morning.

As he got things going in the kitchen, Charlie's thoughts turned towards Denny Caraway, as they often did. It had been over a year since he knew Denny had disappeared off his homestead. Ever since Caraway had brought Gwen out to the homestead, the two of them had come in from the bush every six weeks to two months to check the mail, and to visit Charlie and old man Elliot. Gwen being with him had brought Denny back into the human fold, socializing the man again, after years of solitary living in the bush.

After Gwen became sick and then passed away all too quickly, Denny had shown up that one time, gave Brady his 30-06, nodded to him, and left. It was then Brady knew Gwen was gone, and the last time he had seen Caraway.

Four months after the brief interaction, wondering what was going on with Denny, Charlie got a friend of his who owned a small bush plane to fly him in to the homestead on Lanyard Creek. They found a spot large enough to land the little plane about a quarter mile away. Charlie went walking in and what he saw surprised him, knowing how Denny felt about the place.

The cabin door was wide open and it was obvious bears and other animals had come and wreaked havoc on the place. It was a god-awful mess inside, nothing left intact. There were lots of Denny's clothes and gear torn and scattered around, with broken and bitten foodstuff containers all over the floor. Charlie thought the worst, believing Denny would never leave his place to the animals like this unless something severe had happened to him.

Brady sat down on the wood splitting stump to consider the situation. He decided Denny had either gone elsewhere, not wanting to be on the homestead without Gwen, or he had walked into the forest and taken matters into his own hands. Charlie wouldn't expect that from Caraway, though the last he had seen Denny, the man had seemed totally undone by Gwen's death. Charlie had to find out.

Out of respect for Denny, since the place was a total ruin already, Charlie found some nails and a hammer in the old cabin, nailed the bear boards over the windows, and made sure the door was shut tight, and then left.

When his friend had flown him back in, Charlie called Search and Rescue in Fairbanks, related the situation to them, and requested a search be put into effect. Though he thought it, he didn't suggest that the search might end up being a retrieval.

The search went on for three days, and near the end of the last day, an ATV was spotted about twenty miles to the east of the homestead on the edge of a tundra meadow. When they described it, Charlie knew it was Denny's. The wheeler was in bad shape, the seat and plastic parts all broken and chewed on, and two of the tires flat from being bitten through. Charlie asked that it be choppered in to the North Star Cafe.

There had been no sign of human life or remains, and the search was ended.

Charlie, after some long nights, had concluded Gwen's death had been too much for Denny, and he had intentionally disappeared. He refused to believe Denny had been killed by accident or animal attack. He knew the man too well. But, until such time as some real evidence was found, he wouldn't be sure.

Charlie told Elliot about the situation when he went over to Denny's trailer to sniff around. Elliot told Charlie that Denny had signed the trailer over to him and his grandson, which strengthened Brady's idea of Denny going away on purpose. He shared his thoughts with Elliot.

"I wondered how Gwen's death might affect the man, Mr. Brady. It really tore his heart up, I know that. Please let me know if you hear anything."

Several months later, Elliot passed away, basically from old age. He had already talked to his grandson when he felt he didn't have long, and passed ownership of his own home and the Caraway trailer to him, asking Drew to take care of the place in case Mr. Caraway ever showed up, and return the place to him if he did. The young man loved his granddad and was cut from the same cloth. He promised to take care of things. Since Elliot had left his own house to him, it was a simple matter of walking over to take care of things.

The next six months passed on, as time will do no matter what the human condition might bring. Charlie held the hope Denny might someday come walking in as he used to, and maybe Charlie could talk to him, and help him if it was what Denny needed. Brady knew, having seen the best and worst of human nature, that no one can escape their destiny, and perhaps Denny becoming a sad, possibly demented, human hiding away in the forest from society might be his.

Time passed by, and nothing about Denny came to light, until those moose hunters came into the cafe.

That next fall, when moose season was going strong, three hunters came into the cafe. They definitely looked as if they'd spent time in the willows, hunting the giant creatures. There had been a cold rain mixed with light wet snow falling on and off for days, and these three seemed grateful for the warmth of the cafe and the hot coffee and food they ordered.

Charlie was leaning on the counter, listening to the hunters reliving the hunt, one of them getting his moose. Then, something was mentioned that made Charlie stand up straight, all his senses alert.

"Boy, that sure was a strange looking dude I saw, really scary. I wish you two had seen him. He was something. He looked like somebody out of a crazy-man-in-the-woods movie. I'm glad he went away."

"Yeah, I wish we'd have seen him too. Are you sure you're not just messing with us?"

"You know me better than that. He was really wild with that fur hat he was wearing, but it was the look in his eyes that freaked me out most of all. Never seen such a hard, cold stare, like he could look right through me. I didn't know what he might do. All I did was turn to call you guys and he was gone like a shadow. I'm glad we were packed up to ride back in. I don't think I would have stayed another night out there."

Charlie broke into their conversation, his intense interest in the story startling them. He knew what to ask: where they had been, and what the guy looked like. It was the description of those piercing eyes that made his mind up. Charlie knew it could only be Denny Caraway. The hunters carried GPS tracking devices, so they gave Charlie the coordinates of their camp where the man had been seen.

Charlie once again enlisted the help of his pilot friend to scout the area, two days after he talked to the hunters. Though they searched the specified area for hours, they saw nothing. Charlie decided to let it go, thinking maybe the guy who supposedly saw the "wild man," was simply telling a tale after all. Even if he was telling the truth, the man he saw could be anywhere by now.

Fall evolved into winter. The temperatures dropped and snow fell steadily. Business at the North Star had slowed down by January. Charlie was bored and tired of his own coffee. He decided to take a few days and do a snow machine ride and some winter camping. He enjoyed being out in the winter woods.

He decided there was no better trail to ride than the one along the Salcha River, which eventually ran by Lanyard Creek and the Caraway homestead. Charlie thought it might be a good thing to check the condition of the cabin and who knew, maybe he'd spend the night and clean up the place if no one else had been there already.

Brady put all his gear together and went over his snow machine, checking out its condition. Behind the snow machine in his shop was Denny's wheeler. Charlie had restored the machine to good working condition.

Always keeping his Skidoo in great shape, Charlie packed his gear in the rack and on the rear end of the seat, then went to eat his dinner, get some sleep, and leave in the morning.

Though the day before had been cloudy with snow flurries, the morning was clear, not a cloud in the wintery sky. Brady made note of the extreme change, glad for the good day. Cranking up his machine, Charlie headed out.

He had no trouble following the trail. The work Denny had done on it had made it pretty easy traveling, heading out to Lanyard Creek. It took him about six hours to reach the old homestead, and he arrived before what daylight there was had not yet faded. Opening the door to the cabin, Charlie saw it was still a mess, and was sorry to see no one had cleaned it up.

Going out to his machine to continue on his way before finding a good place to camp for the night, Charlie happened to glance up at the low hill between the cabin and the little lake beyond it. Squinting his eyes against the glare off the snow, Charlie thought he saw some tracks, and walked over to investigate. Sure enough, when he got closer he saw a set of snowshoe tracks leading up to the top of the rise.

Following the tracks, he worked his way up to where the tracks ended, between two birches. Charlie pondered the way the tracks stopped, then continued back down the hill at an angle, and onto the trail again at some distance from the cabin. Whoever had been there had stood in that spot for some specific reason, perhaps looking over the lake, visible from the vantage point. The way the tracks were smeared in the snow made it appear as if whoever it was had stood there a while.

Suddenly, as if a curtain was lifted from his thoughts, Charlie Brady knew without a doubt who had been there and why. He was standing where Gwen Caraway was buried, and it was her husband who had come to visit the grave, not going near the cabin when he did, wanting only to stand over his beloved wife. Charlie got goose bumps all over when he realized the situation, confirming that he was right. Caraway was still around.

Brady followed the tracks down onto the back trail, heading away, deeper into the bush. He decided to follow the tracks, camping when the light gave way to winter darkness.

Running his snow machine at low speed, Charlie followed the tracks for mile after mile. Mostly, the prints avoided the heaviest forest, often running across the numerous tundra meadows. About fifteen miles from the Lanyard Creek homestead, Charlie came across the remains of a simple spruce-bough shelter, and the cold ashes of a small campfire, partly covered with snow. Whoever it was had spent the night there, on the way out and the way back.

When the snowshoe prints finally entered heavy woods, Charlie parked his machine outside the trees, checked his GPS position, and slipped on his bear paw snowshoes and shouldered his pack. He checked his .357 service revolver under his parka and began walking into the trees, following the tracks.

When he got to an area where the trees were dense and the snow not as deep, he took his bear paws off to make walking easier through the undergrowth. He saw no snowshoe tracks, but found some boot prints. Whoever it was had taken off their snowshoes too. Charlie tied his bear paws to his pack and followed the prints.

Charlie had traveled another hundred yards or so when he smelled the undeniable scent of wood smoke. He did something he had learned from his work in the troopers. Whenever he was coming up to a camp where poaching or other illegal activities might be going on, he began whistling. He figured it was something they didn't expect a game officer on the case to be doing, and usually caught them off-guard, making them easier to deal with. He knew it was Denny Caraway he was tracking, but Brady had no idea what his mental condition was at that point.

The smell of smoke got stronger, although he couldn't see a campsite or dwelling. Then, he turned to the right and stood amazed.

There was a very little log cabin, so snugly tucked inside a ring of trees and willows, he wondered how it had been built there, unless it was old enough that the trees had grown up around it. It was a little trapper cabin, barely eight by ten feet in size, with a set of handmade snowshoes leaning against the front wall. There appeared to be no windows, but a small stove pipe was sticking up out of one corner, wisps of the smoke he smelled coming from the stack.

He considered walking up to the hut when suddenly, a familiar voice behind him said, "Officer Brady."

Without turning around, Charlie said, "Mr. Caraway." Charlie stood silently for a moment, then said, "Got any coffee brewing? I could use a cup." Then he turned around.

The sight before him made him do a mental double take, so strange it was. There stood Denny Caraway, looking like a man from another, more primitive time. He was dressed in a fur hat, made from a coyote's head skin, and a down parka, heavily stained, with numerous patches, but with a beautiful ruff made of wolverine fur. His gloves were rabbit skin, the right one off and hanging by a piece of leather lanyard, the bare hand gripping an old lever action Winchester rifle. On his feet were some old pacs which had seen better days. His beard was long and full, and his hair stuck out thickly from under the skin hat.

"Just came to visit, Denny, not to intrude on your solitude. I can leave, if you like." Charlie noticed how lean Denny had become, even in the thick parka. His face looked much thinner too. Still, he looked healthy for all that.

Denny stood staring at him. His intense look seemed even sharper and somehow deeper than before. Charlie was so glad to see his old friend still alive, he couldn't help smiling. Sticking out his hand, he said, "Damn, Denny, it's really good to see you again."

Denny didn't smile, but there was a relenting of the coldness in his eyes. Reaching out, he shook Charlie's hand gently.

"No coffee. I have some Labrador tea."

"That would be fine, thanks."

They went into the tiny cabin, Charlie having to bend down to pass through the low door. There was a small window in the back wall made from a piece of thick plastic sheeting. Once his eyes got used to the dim light, Brady saw there wasn't much inside, only a wooden plank bed with several blankets and a sleeping bag on it, a stump probably used for a chair, a small wooden counter, and several wooden shelves. In one corner was a rusty old sheet metal military woodstove with a cast iron skillet leaning on the wall near the stove. The stove had seen better days and Charlie wondered if it came from the person who had originally built the cabin. There wasn't much by way of foodstuffs in the cabin either. Charlie wondered how Denny was keeping fit.

In fact, he wondered how Denny had survived at all, despite his great store of wilderness knowledge.

It was a meager dwelling by anyone's standards. The thought that came to Charlie's mind was, "Gone to ground; the man has gone to ground."

Denny poured some of the tea into an old heavy mug and handed it to Charlie, then poured some into a handmade wooden cup for himself.

Charlie noticed one shelf with a few personal items on it, including a small photo in a wooden frame of Gwen as a younger woman, smiling and holding up a large salmon she had obviously just caught. Charlie didn't remark on it.

The two old friends didn't talk much about anything, but sat in each other's company. Charlie did ask Denny how he was doing. Denny looked at him a moment and simply said, "As you see me."

After all too brief a time, Charlie knew he should go. He stood, slipped on his gloves, and walked to the door. Denny walked out with him. It was then Charlie saw the several moose quarters hanging high up by a rope in a tree, safe from any marauding critters, and hard to spot by people, too.

"Well, take care, Denny, and if you ever see your way clear, I'd be happy to stake you to a meal and all the coffee you want at the cafe." Then Charlie added, "There are some people wishing the best for you, Denny."

Denny stood a moment, then nodded slightly. Charlie nodded too, and began walking back the way he had come. He looked back once, but Denny was gone. Turning away again, Charlie left, a pain in his heart from seeing his friend in such condition.

Brady put his snowshoes back on and walked out to his snow machine as the light was failing. He decided not to camp despite the late hour, rode back past Denny's old homestead, and continued on to the highway and normal life, though Charlie felt nothing would feel quite the same to him after his meeting with Denny.

He feared Denny was truly lost to the world, and would remain a sad, lonely hermit until something in the wilderness put him out of his obvious misery. Charlie mentally kicked himself for his negative thoughts, for giving up on Caraway. He felt he still knew the man, and just had to keep thinking one day he'd show up at the cafe, have that free meal and coffee, and get on with life.

Charlie knew when wild creatures are sick or wounded, they often go to ground, hide away to lick their wounds and heal until they are well enough to continue the eternal battle of survival. He hoped Denny would heal. Brady was a skookum man.

Chapter Twenty Eight

After Charlie left him, Denny took a walk in the trees. His mind was in turmoil. Charlie's visit, though Denny was glad to see him, had stirred up sore emotions Caraway had laid to rest, or thought he had, by going deep, living in total isolation. Except for being spotted by a moose hunter the previous fall, Caraway had seen no one all the time he had been there.

Denny thought back on his recent life. As his initial, meager supplies ran out, Denny used his hard-learned woods lore to survive. He caught, shot, and gathered whatever he needed to keep going. It had all made him stronger, but always there was the hole in his middle where Gwen used to be.

Recently, he had actually begun asking God for guidance and help to survive the grief he felt. Though not a religious man, Denny needed something to keep his self-exile from overwhelming his mind. Several times, a small incident made him wonder if his asking for help had actually made a difference.

One morning, he walked out into a nearby tundra meadow while hunting for a moose. His supply of meat had completely run out and he'd not seen any moose for some time. Denny paused and asked for a moose to keep body and soul together. A few minutes later, a young bull moose had walked out into the meadow, not even fifty feet from where he was, and stood looking at him. Denny was surprised. This was not typical behavior, an animal presenting itself as if it were waiting. Then, the moose stood broadside to him, looking away. Amazed, Denny took careful aim, shot the heavy caliber old rifle, and the moose collapsed to the ground, the bullet finding its heart. Denny walked over to the animal, perfect for his needs, looked up, and said, "Thank you."

Brady's visit might be a sign. Searching his heart, Denny decided it was time to return to life, the life of other people, of troubles and joys, of challenges, and moments of contentment. When he had the realization, it felt as if a great weight had been lifted.

Going into his shelter, he saw it differently now. At first he had planned to live there until his last days. Now, he knew it had been a place to lay up in, until his mind and heart had healed, until Gwen's death was bearable. Perhaps now, after living this solitary existence for so long, it was time to look forward and accept — a time to return.

That night, Denny slept longer and deeper than he had in all the time he had lived there. When he awoke the next morning and went outside, he saw there was a set of wolf prints leading up to the shelter, going around it several times and then leading off in the general direction he would take to get back to Lanyard Creek.

He had taken a long hike many years ago, and it had set him on a new path in life. Now, he would take another long walk, not into the unknown, but back to the best home he'd ever had.

Denny went out to where the moose meat was hanging. He lowered the frozen meat down, sawed off a few nice pieces, and carried the rest out into the trees for animals to eat, rather than let it hang out of reach until it spoiled in warmer weather.

It only took him a few minutes to gather up what he had in the crude dwelling. Hoisting his pack and taking up the old rifle, his wife's old rifle, once again, he simply walked away.

It took him several days to get back to Lanyard Creek. He made a simple shelter for the night he stayed out, spruce boughs for a bed, poles and spruce boughs overhead, and a cleared space for a small fire to reflect its heat into his shelter. It was a cold, clear, beautiful night. Caraway realized he hadn't seen the beauty around him for a long time. As Denny lay there in his down bag looking at the stars, he felt himself filling up again, his spirit being renewed.

The next afternoon, he arrived at Lanyard Creek. There was enough light for him to see his old home. Denny paused for a long minute to look at what he once was determined would be his last homestead, refusing to let anything run him off, until Gwen's death had changed everything. Standing there, Denny knew he had come home, even though Gwen was gone. His heart filled with the long-denied feeling of happiness in being back where he truly belonged.

Denny turned and walked up the little rise where his wife was buried. Standing over her resting place, Denny stood there until darkness came. "I've come home, Gwen," he said. Then he walked back down to the homestead.

Denny saw the cabin had been closed up, though he knew he had left it open. One name came to mind. "Charlie."

Walking up to the sturdy cabin, he saw there were some deep claw marks on the solid door, the heavy framing within keeping even a hungry bear from breaking it down.

Reaching up to the top of the outer door frame, he felt for and found the spruce wood handle to the latch. Sliding it in the slot, he pushed to the left and opened the door.

It was dark inside, but he walked to where the kerosene lamp had always hung, his feet kicking things lying on the floor. The lamp was still there. Denny had to search around on the shelf where he had kept small items, and finally found the plastic baggie with a small box of matches in it, and lit the lantern.

As the flame heightened, he saw the incredible mess his cabin had been become. It reminded him of the way his original homestead had looked when he had first arrived there after it had been deserted for five years.

Slowly shaking his head, Denny said, "Damn bears."

Finis

Other Books By Warren Troy

Can a middle-aged urban dwelling man survive on his own in the Alaska wilderness? Denny Caraway is going to find out. Casting off city life that has become completely unsatisfying--that is killing his spirit--he journeys north to become a homesteader in the Alaska bush. Denny is pushed to his limits, physically and spiritually, while carving out a life in the trees, experiencing daily adventures that could end his life if he doesn't make the right choices. Despite the danger, he comes to love his new home and almost everything involved there. But he learns that bad human behavior is everywhere, as he deals with neighboring Alaskan homesteaders. After the peace and solitude of his homestead life is threatened, Denny must make life-changing decisions to maintain his cherished freedom.

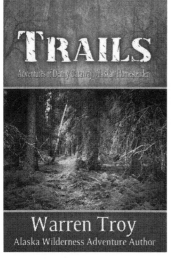

An inexperienced teenager leaves his suburban California home to visit his brother in San Francisco, and dives into the Hippie Movement of the sixties.

Establishing himself in the Flower Power scene of the Haight Ashbury District, he becomes a bell-bottomed entrepreneur, running a unique used garment business from the back of an old, brightly painted step van, becoming known only as Jester.

Heavily involved in the sex, drugs and rock and roll lifestyle, he meets fascinating characters like Janis Joplin and Timothy Leary and has many amazing experiences, until he burns out on the whole scene. Leaving the bay area, He searches for a different direction.

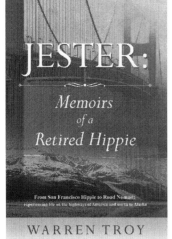

Jester moves in and out of different lifestyles, becoming a road nomad, traveling, over the years, from the mountains of Big Sur all the way to Alaska, with many stops along the way. In Jester: Memoirs of a Retired Hippie, Jester tastes love and loss, joy and deep sorrow, and the magic that still exists in the world, evolving into a unique and wise older man.

Made in the USA
Charleston, SC
07 February 2013